A CURIOUS PLACE

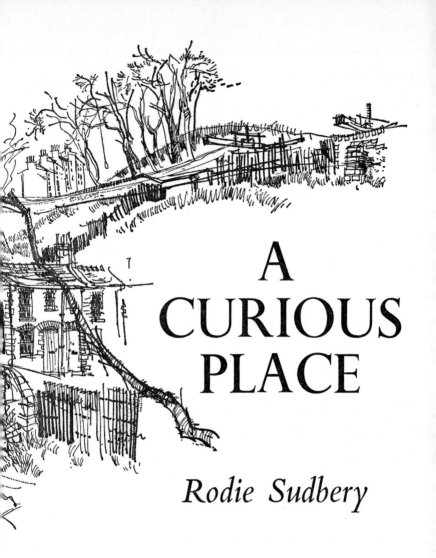

A
CURIOUS
PLACE

Rodie Sudbery

ANDRE DEUTSCH

First published 1973 by
André Deutsch Limited
105 Great Russell Street London WC1

Printed in Great Britain
by Ebenezer Baylis and Son Ltd
The Trinity Press Worcester and London

ISBN 0 233 96405 3

For my sister Jenny

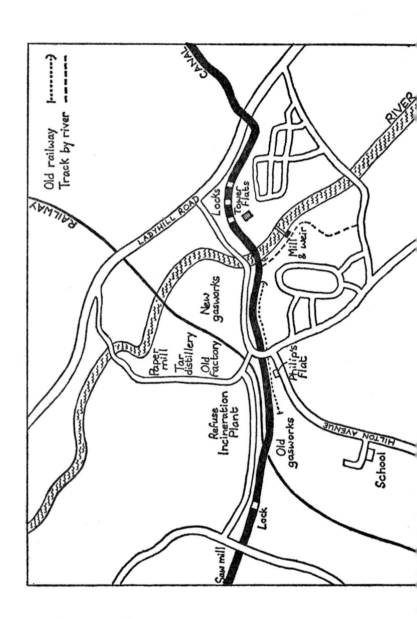

Old railway [·······>
Track by river ------

CANAL

RIVER

RAILWAY

LADYHILL ROAD

Locks

Tower
Flats

Mill
& weir

Paper
mill

Tar
distillery

Old
Factory

New
gasworks

Philip's
Flat

Refuse
Incineration
Plant

Old
gasworks

HILTON AVENUE

School

Lock

Saw mill

One

'I don't suppose we'll notice the factory much,' said Mr Gray.

'It's right in the middle of the view,' said Mrs Gray. 'If you can call it a view. How you could have missed it when you were looking over the flat I simply don't understand.'

'I was concentrating on the gasworks. You can't see them at all. One lot's too far to the right and the other's too far to the left.'

'You can see them if you lean out of the window,' said Martha helpfully.

'You're not to lean out of the window. It isn't safe,' said her mother. Although the flat was ground floor at the front the back garden was ten feet down.

'I didn't,' said Martha. 'Philip told me.'

'Philip isn't to lean out either. Do you hear me, Philip?'

'Yes.'

'There you are, John, that's something we'll have to fix,' said Mrs Gray to her husband, 'bars on the bedroom windows.'

Philip thought it was a silly idea. Martha's bedroom at home didn't have bars – he corrected himself: hadn't had bars.

It was awfully hard to remember that this was home now, not the house in Grantham. He didn't mind sharing a room with Martha; he had been surprised, not indignant, when told he would have to in the small flat; but he certainly would mind if it meant bars at the window.

'It must be quite a new factory,' said Mr Gray. 'It isn't marked on the map.'

It looked new, Philip thought; its metal parts were so bright they hurt his eyes, and there was a sheer wall of dazzling whiteness. No smoke was coming from the one tall chimney.

'If it's new they're probably going to build it a whole lot bigger,' said Mrs Gray.

'At least it's some way away.'

Between them and the factory was first the shared back garden; then the floor of the valley, all wild greenness across to the road on the opposite hillside; then ground that could only be guessed at, because the factory appeared to lie next to the road, but in fact couldn't – not judging from the size of the tiny man walking about on the roof. Philip watched the cars on the road. Two dust lorries crawled along; squat silvery things of modern enclosed design, slightly sinister if you didn't know what they were: there might be anything inside.

'Well,' said Mr Gray, pushing his chair back from the breakfast table, 'I must be getting along.'

'You're not going in to the office today?' cried his wife. 'What about all the things you were going to fix?'

'They'll have to wait until this evening.'

'It'll be awfully difficult to unpack. There's nowhere to put *anything* – I never saw a place so short of storage space.'

'Well, we'll only be here until we find something better.'

'What about the four months' lease?'

'I told you, there was no way out of that. In any case it may well take us four months to look round. We don't want to choose in a hurry.'

'We certainly don't. Not again.'

'Are you going to unpack soon, Mummy?' asked Martha, and not being instantly answered went on: 'Are you going to unpack soon? You are going to unpack soon, aren't you, Mummy? I want to help you.'

'You see what it will be like! How can I possibly get anything done? Surely they won't expect you at work today, after that awful journey yesterday?'

'Look, dear, it isn't a matter of what they expect. I was very fortunate to get this job; it's up to me now. Why don't you let the children go out for a walk?'

'Yes, would you like to?' said Philip to Martha, who was looking indignant and hurt. He would really have preferred to go by himself, but he thought this wasn't the moment to say so. With or without Martha, he wanted very much to see what ran along the bottom of the valley. He couldn't understand why his mother didn't like this view; to him it was full of interest, drawing him irresistibly to explore. The view from the front window was depressing, certainly: blocks of flats stuck together in grey sameness all the way down the road. The flats opposite were at the top of a high bank and filled most of the sky. Here at the back there was plenty of sky; and clouds, and sunshine, and space.

Philip and Martha left the house with their father, and while he drove off in the car they walked to the nearby end of the road. He turned up the steep hill, and they went the other way, on to the bridge Philip had seen from the window; bridges, rather, because the valley bottom was quite wide. First they crossed a disused railway cutting, deep and overgrown; then there was a canal, and finally a proper permanent way with two sets of shining rails. They waited here until rewarded by a train, Philip with one arm round Martha's plump waist as they leaned across the parapet.

'Now shall we go along by the canal?' he said, and they

turned back to where they had passed the entrance to the tow-path. The path was divided from the disused railway cutting by a high fence; on the far side of the railway cutting were the back gardens of the flats.

'I wonder which is ours? If Mummy looked out we could wave,' said Philip.

'Let's call to her,' said Martha.

'No, better not.' They would have to scream at the tops of their voices to have any chance of being heard, and she was probably busy unpacking. The flat might look quite different when they got back, particularly if they stayed out a good long while. Their mother might be in a better mood, too.

The path was rough and gritty. They walked on the grass at the side and Martha picked flowers: clover and dandelions and something Philip thought might be ragged robin. They passed the gasworks, holding their breath against the bitter choking smell.

'Look,' said Martha, 'a car in the water.'

'There can't be.' But there was; rusty and windowless, submerged as far as its roof.

'Do you think they drove it in by mistake? Do you think they're all drowned?'

Philip considered the possibility of a set of skeletons sitting inside. 'No,' he said finally. 'I expect somebody didn't want it any more.'

They passed two small round willows covered in catkins. There were many more on the opposite bank, their branches leaning out over the canal, pale spots of catkins reflected in the water. Martha wanted to pick some but the stems were too tough for her. Philip helped.

The canal curved.

'I think we're coming to a lock,' said Philip.

'What's a lock?'

'A sort of step in the water.' He wondered if he could possibly explain its workings to her.

When they got nearer he realized this one hadn't worked for some time. It was permanently closed at both ends. Water trickled through a hole in the top gates in a steady stream, and must get out somewhere at the other end, because the lock was practically dry. The bottom was strewn with rubbish. Philip had never seen such large objects thrown away before. There was a mattress, an old zinc bath with handles, two buckets, a sink, and the upholstered back seat of a car. There was also a football which, though dirty, looked perfectly good. 'I expect that went in by mistake,' said Philip.

'Couldn't they get it out?' Martha's eyes grew round as she pictured the unknown owners' distress.

'No.' Actually there was a rusty ladder on the far side, but Philip didn't think anybody would want to make the descent against the slimy black stones.

They left the lock after a while. The path wound down, steep and stony, until they reached the lower level below the lock. There was a house with a small front garden; it must once have been the lock-keeper's cottage, and now seemed to belong to a dealer in used cars.

There was another lock and then the canal was crossed by a road. It was dark under the bridge, with a big puddle in the middle of the path which looked as if it never dried. They edged past it on the wall side. The iron structure drummed to the sound of cars passing overhead. DANGER: SUBMARINE CABLE said a notice; and it took Philip some time to work out that the warning was addressed to the barges which no longer came this way.

Beyond the bridge they passed stacks of timber, enormous rough-hewn planks with splits in their ends. There was a saw-mill across the canal. They played here for a while, climbing and jumping. One of the giant planks floated in the water, edge upwards like a long black roof.

There was a way up to the road and Philip decided to take it. However long they followed the canal they would always want to see what lay round the next bend, and if they turned back here they could go a different way home. They crossed the bridge and found a turning which he hoped was the road he had seen from the back windows of the flat.

Though narrow, the road was quite busy. It had no pavement, and most of the way no verge either. Martha was supposed to be walking on the inside, but she wiggled about and Philip continually had to grab her as cars whizzed unexpectedly round the nearest bend.

The road sloped up between trees until they came into the open just where Philip had hoped they would be, across the valley from their flat. It was even more impossible to pick out which was theirs from here. Between them lay the railway cutting, deep and wide; then the canal, then the towpath, then the old railway. Lines of houses rose one behind the other up the far hill, their road and the road beyond it and the road beyond that, all the way to the top. They made stripes, paler and paler as they receded. Did the dirt come from the railway, wondered Philip, or the gasworks? Their own block was very dark indeed.

'I'm tired,' said Martha; then with pleased recognition: 'That looks like where we live.'

'It is,' said Philip, rather impressed.

'It looks a long way.'

'It isn't really. You'll see.' They turned the corner on to the railway bridge where they had watched for trains.

When they got in they found nothing much had changed. The table by the window at which they had eaten breakfast was still an oasis of normality in a room full of tea-chests.

'What can I have to put my flowers in?' asked Martha.

'Oh dear, I don't know,' said their mother. 'Philip, you find her something.'

He went into the kitchen.

'Just look at your hands!' she continued on a sharper note. 'What on earth have you been doing?'

'Only picking flowers.'

'Everything's filthy, I suppose – it must be the atmosphere. Well, go and wash as soon as you've finished messing about with those.'

Philip returned with a mug.

'I rang your school,' said his mother. 'I had to go and find a kiosk; they said they'd connect our telephone this morning, but they haven't done it yet. The headmaster wants to see you next Monday, Philip. You start next Tuesday.'

'When do I start?' asked Martha.

'Oh yes, that's another thing. They can't take Martha until next term.'

She began to wail. 'I want to go to school with Philip! Why can't I go to school?'

'They do things differently in Glasgow.'

'I don't want to live in Glasgow,' wept Martha.

'I don't particularly want to live here either. We shall just have to make the best of it. Philip, I'd like you to go down the road to the shops for me. I forgot to buy any butter.'

Martha went with Philip, still quietly snuffling her disappointment at not starting school. Philip felt a bit sorry as well. His first day might have been easier in some ways with Martha to escort. It would have given him a definite task, and prevented him feeling nervous on his own account.

The flats marched down the road without a break, except for a patch of waste ground beside the gasworks. Each entrance was the same, pale stone steps and tiled walls, but the tiny front gardens were all different. A cat slept on the sill outside one window, and outside another perched a Scotch terrier.

There were half a dozen shops in a row. One sold fish and chips. A crowd of boys came out of it, about Philip's age. There was a single boy looking in the newsagent's window and they reached out to tousle his hair. He ducked as though the same thing had happened many times before. Philip pulled Martha quickly into the grocer's, and wondered if the boys went to his new school.

Going back up the road Martha stared with interest at each group of children playing on the pavement.

'Who will be my friends here?' she asked Philip.

'I don't know. You'll have to see.'

She thought friends were her right. Philip chiefly wanted people to leave him alone. He had left one friend in Grantham, John Eccles, an undemanding boy. Stolid, some people called him, whereas they called Philip shy. He and John had decided this was because John was thick and sturdy, while Philip was small for his age and slight.

They recognized their entrance by Philip's bicycle just inside at the bottom of the stairs. It was a good place for it so long as nobody objected. The staircase served six flats, three each side, but he seemed to be the only person with a bike. There was a cold institutional feel to the echoing stone steps and tiled walls.

Lunch wasn't ready yet, so they went to explore the back garden which the six flats shared. Opening a heavy door they found the back steps in a dark cleft of the building. They were gritty with coaldust and had slippery moss at their edges.

The garden was mostly grass. There were iron clothes posts, one pair for each flat, with lines strung between or neatly coiled. Against the wall of the building people kept coal, in containers that varied from a smart concrete bunker to a rusty bath. Philip and Martha went to the bottom of the garden and looked through the high fence at the overgrown railway cutting.

Then Martha noticed two children in the garden next door,

and rushed to the side fence to get a better view. There was a tiny girl with dark curls and a shrill voice, and another about the same size as Martha. They paid no attention to her. Presently Philip felt he ought to go over and entice her away.

'That one's called Alison and that one's called Joan,' she told him.

'Don't point. Let's go and see if the meal's ready.'

'No, I want to watch them.'

The small dark-haired one – Alison – raised her head from her doll's pram and caught Philip's eye. He smiled and said 'Hallo'.

'What's your name?' she asked.

'Philip. And Martha,' he said, answering for Martha because he could see she was tongue-tied.

'Have you come to live next door?'

'Yes.'

'I saw you playing,' Martha got out.

'I know you did,' said Alison.

There was a shout from the next door back steps and a boy appeared.

'Alison! You've to come in and get your dinner!'

Alison turned and ran.

'That's Gordon,' whispered Joan before she trailed after.

Philip thought the boy had been the leader of the group who came out of the fish and chip shop. He wasn't sure.

Two

Two days later there was no bread for breakfast. Philip's mother said she hadn't got the shopping organised yet.

'There's no baker's down the road, but I think they have rolls.'

'Fresh rolls for breakfast. That sounds good,' said Mr Gray.

'I'll go on my bike,' said Philip. Martha was still in her pyjamas, so there was no question of her coming too.

He unlocked the bike and then found he had two flat tyres. After trying vainly to connect his pump he realised that someone had taken his valves.

He relocked the bike, thought for a moment and removed the front light. Running up the six steps to their front door he left light and pump just inside the flat before setting off on foot.

He had forgotten to ask which shop had the rolls, but he found that apart from the hairdresser's and the launderette they all did. He bought his from the butcher's.

When he got back his mother was standing in the doorway holding the milk and talking to the lady in the flat across the stairs.

'You were a long time,' she said.

Philip explained why.

'Took your *valves*?'

'Nothing would surprise me round here,' said Mrs Macleod. (Philip supposed this must be her name; it was printed on her letterbox.) 'You're lucky they didn't take the whole bike.'

'It was locked.'

Martha sidled round the door and her mother said: 'Will you go and get some clothes on? Hurry up and don't let me have to tell you again!'

'You'll catch a nasty chill,' said Mrs Macleod. Martha eyed her cautiously, standing on one leg.

'Now the rolls are here we'd better have breakfast.' Sweeping them both inside Mrs Gray shut the door.

'Meeting the neighbours?' asked their father.

'She told me where to buy the whitening for the steps,' their mother said helplessly. 'Whitening! I didn't think it existed. Oh, and if I want to hang the washing out on a Sunday nobody will mind.'

'Nice to know,' said Mr Gray, winking at Philip. 'Are those the rolls? I can smell them from here. Let's get at them.'

Mrs Gray told him about Philip's missing valves.

'Really? What a nuisance! I wonder who took those.'

Philip had intended to go out exploring on his bicycle that morning. He went for a walk instead, and as there was no sign of Alison or Joan Martha came too. They crossed all the bridges and took the road that went straight up across the corner of the hill. They passed the entrance to the factory. Its chimney was sending out white smoke; 'steam, mostly,' Philip's father had said at breakfast, 'look, it's invisible where it starts.'

'REFUSE INCINERATION PLANT', read Philip. That explained all the dust lorries. He had counted thirteen the day before while they ate their tea. He thought it was a good thing their mother had been able to see the cleanness of the smoke before finding out what it came from.

On the other side of the road were the crumbling buildings of a factory that had been abandoned. Rubbish had been pushed through a brick archway to make a great pile where the ground fell away. Above the old washing machines and sofas with protruding springs the arch framed a view of Glasgow: tenements crowding the sides of a distant hill, and a slender white block of modern flats towering behind.

The road was narrow and winding. It was a country lane that had been captured by the city. Dandelions blazed on the littered verges; a sheet of torn polythene hung in the branches of a silver birch. On one bend steps led down to an old cottage tucked between a tar distillery and a paper mill, an enormous chimney rising almost out of its roof. The paper mill collected old paper, bales and bales of it stacked in a strange whitish landscape that stretched as far as the children could see. The road sloped down more steeply and all of a sudden they were crossing a river, shallow and stony with cliffs on one side.

'This must be the one on the map,' said Philip.

Beyond the bridge their way climbed until it joined a main road. Philip looked at the streaming traffic and said they would go back the way they had come. Martha looked at the shops and said she wanted an ice cream.

'Oh all right. I'll have one too.' The nearest sweet shop wasn't far.

They were soon back at the river with a long climb ahead of them. They trudged past the paper mill, the little cottage, the tar distillery, and came to the abandoned factory where they rested for a while, leaning against the sides of an open gateway.

'Let's go in,' said Martha.

Philip didn't see why not. His feet were tired of the rough stony road. 'Come on then,' he said.

He looked about with interest as they picked their way past tumbledown sheds and old railway sidings.

'Oh!' said Martha. 'There's Gordon!'

At the same moment Philip realised they were not alone. He recognised in the distance the gang of boys he had seen by the shops. Alison's brother Gordon was among them; he had heard Martha's shout.

'It's all right,' Philip heard him tell the others, 'we needn't worry about them.'

They laughed. They were all over the buildings, climbing like monkeys, peering from glassless upper storey windows.

'Can we do that?' said Martha.

'No,' said Philip. He really wanted to withdraw immediately, but that would have looked like running away. Undecided, he walked a little further. The sheds weren't so dilapidated here. Then he saw one that was sticky with new paint, paint cans and brushes lying on the ground beside it.

'Look here,' he said, stopping and gazing ahead, 'we're coming to the tar distillery, I think. All this must belong to them.'

Questions of ownership meant little to Martha. Philip, however, decreed that they should turn back. They had already done so when the man appeared; a man in a dirty white boilersuit who shouted: 'Hey there!'

Philip noticed the boys were running away. Martha would have liked to do the same, but he held her firmly by the hand. 'I don't like that cross man,' she whimpered.

Another man had appeared in the path of the running boys, and they were turning back. The first man reached Philip. He seemed a little surprised to find him stationary. 'What are you doing in here?' he asked.

'We just came in to have a look. We're sorry,' said Philip.

'This is private property. Didn't you know that?' He looked

from Philip to the other boys, now standing in a panting group a few yards away. 'Are you all together?'

'Yes,' said Gordon.

'We're sorry. We didn't know,' said Philip.

The man looked again from Philip and Martha to Gordon and his friends; shook his head and said impatiently: 'Away with you then. And remember I don't want to see you in here again.'

The children went out the way they had come in.

'You did fine,' said Gordon to Philip. 'Lucky for us you were there.' And he grinned in such a fashion that it was impossible not to respond, even when the group fell apart and Philip saw one boy in the middle triumphantly clutching a can of paint. It was a spray can; they tried it out on the wall.

'Do you want a shot?' Gordon asked Philip.

'I want to try it!' said Martha, as Philip hesitated.

'Give it her, Neil.'

'She's too wee,' objected the boy who had stolen the paint.

'No, go on; let her have a shot.'

Philip found himself helping Martha to control the can.

'Do you come from England?' asked one of the boys.

'Yes.'

'They're staying in the next close to us,' said Gordon.

A close must mean a staircase and the flats off it, Philip decided. But staying?

'We're living there.'

'That's what I said. What'll your school be?'

'The one down the road.' Philip had forgotten its name.

'That's ours too.'

They reached the canal bridge and Gordon brandished the paint can at the wall where the towpath led away to the left. (Philip had not explored in this direction yet.) He wrote GORDON DOWNIE OK.

Philip thought that if the men from the factory saw that,

they would know who had taken the paint. The one who hadn't shouted at the children had seemed to be the one who was actually doing the painting; he'd looked a rough sort of person, who could shout plenty if he wanted.

Outside Gordon's close Alison and Joan were playing, and Martha ran towards them.

'Come on,' said Gordon, when Philip would have continued to his flat alone.

'Where?' asked Philip.

'Our back green.'

They went through the middle of the building, up the front steps and down the back.

'Who's got any money?' asked Gordon.

They felt in their pockets, displaying the result on their palms. Philip found himself producing a two penny piece.

'We'll have some chips. The shop'll be open now.'

'Who's a fast runner?' said the boy called Neil.

'He's got a bike,' said Gordon.

They all looked at Philip. 'I'm afraid I can't ride it at the moment,' he began.

Gordon's hand was in his pocket again. 'You can now,' he said, and brought out two valves.

As he pumped up his tyres Philip wondered why he didn't feel more indignant. It was, of course, nice to get the valves back; but more than that, when Gordon had handed them over it had somehow been an important moment.

He jumped on to the bicycle and pedalled away. Behind him Martha was yelling indignantly because of something Alison had said or done. She had already stopped asking who her friends would be. Philip thought a trifle nervously that now he might not need to ask the same question.

Three

'You'd better make the most of this meat,' said Philip's mother, ladling out stew, 'because seeing what it costs up here I shouldn't think we'll be having it very often.'

Philip thought he would have enjoyed it more if she hadn't spoken. It was a pretty ordinary stew; the meat, whatever it had cost, was tougher than usual.

As they were clearing their plates someone banged on the door.

'Go and tell them we haven't finished lunch yet, Philip, and don't let anyone in. Martha, stay where you are. I didn't say you could get down.'

Philip found Alison and Joan standing on the doormat. They were both too small to reach the bell.

'Can Martha come and play?'

Philip repeated his mother's message, advised them to mind their fingers, and closed the door. Martha said she didn't want any pudding, and was given a small helping.

Outside the window the chimney of the refuse incineration plant was puffing innocent white smoke. Round to the right another chimney low on the skyline was producing smoke of extreme blackness which spread into the sky like ink. Philip recognised the chimney by its square shape; it belonged to the tar distillery, and he was surprised to find it visible from the flat. He didn't think his mother had noticed it yet.

There were bangs at the door again.

'Philip, *go* and tell them – '

'I've finished,' said Martha urgently, 'I don't want the rest of my pudding, I'm full right up to here, please can I play?'

Their mother frowned. 'All right,' she said. 'But don't go vanishing inside someone else's house or I shan't be able to call you when it's time for your programme.'

Martha's programme was 'Listen With Mother'. She was always broken-hearted if she missed it. Philip let her out and came back to the table.

'Did Daddy tell you he'd noticed a bicycle shop on his way to work?' asked his mother. 'He said he'd stop and get you some new valves today, if he had time.'

'Oh! Well, my old ones have come back actually,' said Philip.

'You mean they're back on the bike?'

'Yes.'

'How extraordinary!'

'Still, it won't matter if Daddy does get some. It'll be handy to have spares.'

'In case it happens again?'

'Oh, I don't think it will – but they do wear out sometimes – but anyway if I've got spares it won't matter even if it does.'

He filled his mouth with pudding to prevent himself talking any more, and his mother left the subject. It had been an awkward moment.

He was helping to clear the table when they heard feet stamping up the front steps, accompanied by familiar howls. 'Oh what *now*,' sighed Mrs Gray, and opened the front door at the same moment as Mrs Macleod opposite. Martha stood there, her face plastered with tears.

'I want my programme!'

'You can have your programme,' said her mother, exasperated. 'It isn't even time for it yet, so why are you making all this fuss?'

'Well, Alison says I'm not getting it!'

'Oh Martha. She's only teasing you! You really will have to learn not to get so upset, won't you?'

'She's a wee scamp, that one,' said Mrs Macleod. 'But you mustn't let her make you cry, you know. The more you cry the more she'll tease. Isn't that right?'

'Mmm,' sniffed Martha, hypnotised by Mrs Macleod's wheedling tone.

'It's not as though you weren't the bigger. Why, you're far bigger than her! Sure you'll be at school next week and then she won't be able to bother you. I expect she'll miss you then.'

'No, they won't let Martha go until September. She's only just five,' said her mother.

'Oh, I took her for six.'

'She's big for her age.'

'And what about Philip?'

So she knew his name already. 'I'm eleven.'

'And you're small for it! You two ought to be the other way round, didn't you?'

'I'm a midget,' said Philip politely, and slipped away down the steps.

Outside he met Gordon and the other boys. He knew their names now: Robert Lachlan, Alastair Macdonald, Malcolm Drummond, Neil Stuart and his brother James. 'Like the king,' Philip had said, but had received a blank look from James. The Stuart brothers made a unit by themselves, tending to rebel against Gordon, particularly in the matter of having Philip in the gang.

They were bound for the canal and turned right when they reached it, the way Philip hadn't gone yet. They passed GORDON DOWNIE OK.

'Why OK?' asked Philip.

James cast his eyes upward and Gordon said: 'That means it's our territory.'

The canal curved beside them, glassy smooth. Tree tops showed above the wall of crumbling pink cement that separated the towpath from the old cutting. Then the cutting ran into a hill. Led by Gordon they climbed the wall where some stones were missing, went down the steep grassy bank and dropped four feet on to the old line. Philip felt the jolt all the way up his backbone. There were no signs of rails or sleepers, though a few planks lying beside the open mouth of the tunnel suggested a barricade erected by authority and since broken down. Somewhere in the darkness water dripped.

'Who's got any matches?' Gordon asked.

Robert had matches. He didn't strike one until they were a little way in. The ground was uneven and everyone bumped and barged, breathing noisily and laughing a lot.

'Watch out for rats,' said James.

'Watch out for bats,' said Neil.

'Watch out for ghosts!' said Gordon. The match went out, leaving them in what seemed for an instant like total blackness. Something cold fell on the back of Philip's neck. They turned and raced for the daylight behind them.

Philip touched the back of his neck and found it wet. Only a drop of water. Although the sun didn't strike into the cutting it was warm after the tunnel.

'Does it go far?' he asked.

'You can't get much farther. It's blocked.'

Getting out of the cutting was harder than getting in. Gordon stood on Robert's back to reach the grass at the top of the wall. Then he pulled Robert up after him. Each in turn pulled the one behind until only the Stuarts and Philip were left. James hoisted Neil, and then they both stood looking down at Philip. He waited for one of them to kneel and stretch an arm, but neither did. The others were already over the broken wall at the top of the bank.

'I say . . .' If they had decided not to help him he was afraid asking would make no difference.

'He wants up,' said James.

'He'll not be able to manage by himself,' agreed Neil.

Philip looked along the cutting. If he pushed his way through the bushes and under the road, would he be able to climb out by his own garden, or if not shout for help?

'What are you at?' called Gordon, reappearing by the gap in the wall.

'It's this wee lad, he's not very good at climbing.' James and Neil reached for him together so that between them he came up very fast and grazed his knees.

'Come on,' said Gordon.

The others were waiting a few yards further on, where half-way down the bank beside the towpath a large tree grew. Under its roots were cool grassy hollows; on the top half of the bank the soil was bare and shiny. Hanging from one of the branches was a piece of rope with a loop at the end.

Gordon climbed to the top of the bank and fished for the rope with a dead branch. He pulled it towards him and got a good grip on the loop. Then he was running down the bank. As he came level with the tree, where the shelving ground grew steeper, he gave a sort of kick and launched into mid-air on the end of the rope. Philip ducked as he passed over their heads, right out over the canal and back again. He was ready for the earthy part of the bank and gave it one good kick that sent him on another outward swing. Philip saw now why the earth was so bare. When Gordon had had enough he let his feet drag instead of kicking, and after a couple of swings had slowed down enough to grab for the trunk of the tree with one hand and bring himself to a halt beside it.

'Philip now,' said Gordon.

'Why him?' began James, until Neil nudged him. 'Yes, him!' they said together.

'I don't know if I can do it,' Philip faltered.

'Och, it's easy,' said Gordon, 'come on. It's great, you don't want to miss it.'

Philip was sure he would rather miss it, but could not think how to say so to Gordon. He found himself scrambling up the bank; being pushed and pulled over the last slippery inches. He had to stand on tiptoe to reach the rope when it was hooked towards him. He wobbled precariously at the top of the slope, looking down under the branches of the tree to the shining canal and not daring to move.

'What are you waiting for?' said James.

'Go on,' said Gordon, and shoved him firmly in the back.

He lost his balance. He was leaning, falling down the slope, his hands clutching grimly at the rope, his feet running of their own accord. And then there was no more ground to run on; he was swinging out, out, over the towpath, over the canal.

All he wanted was to stop, but he couldn't remember how Gordon had managed it. Although his feet tried instinctively to cling to the bank when they met it on the backward swing he was shorter than Gordon and the soles of his shoes barely scraped the earth. As he swung out again he shut his eyes and tried to think of nothing but holding on. His arms were aching and the rope hurt his hands, but he thought he didn't go quite as far that time. If he did nothing to make himself move perhaps he would stop soon.

'He's too small to kick off,' said James, 'he needs a push.'

'No!' shrieked Philip, as the push sent him speeding faster.

'Don't,' said Gordon to James. 'He's had enough for a first try.'

When at last the rope did slow down Philip couldn't bring himself to let go. 'Stop! Stop!' they all shouted each time he passed the tree, until Gordon came sliding impatiently down the bank and grabbed him by the waist. The solid ground was so easily regained that he felt completely foolish.

He waited on the towpath while the others took turns with the rope. There was a sort of succulent clover growing, grey-green leaves like cat's ears and big dark red blooms. He might have picked some if he had been alone. Away in the distance was the Ladyhill road with its sandstone tenements and flashing cars. It was the main road he had reached with Martha the other day. In between was a stretch of low-lying ground spiked with chimneys; familiar tar distillery chimneys in the distance, pale oddly-spiralled chimneys of the new gasworks in the foreground. These gasworks were very busy, particularly at night, when they made a humming noise and bright lights illuminated clouds of steam. The river must be somewhere down there, though he couldn't see it. The railway embankment cut across straight and high; as he watched a train glided from one end to the other, almost soundless in the distance.

'Do you want another shot?'

'No thanks,' said Philip, and they went on.

The canal turned towards the Ladyhill road. A rutted track led off to one side, shadowed by giant beeches. The towpath had a sort of parapet and Philip looked over and gasped.

Far beneath him was the river. He was on a bridge built to carry the canal over the valley. Across the river was a steep green slope crowned by a twenty-storey block of flats. All down the slope children were playing, looking like bright beads spilled from a bottle.

The whole view was so surprising it took Philip's breath away. It was the best moment of the afternoon.

Four

Philip was walking home. The term was a week old now; long enough for him to have got used to the school. It wasn't very different from his English one, despite some of the dire predictions he had heard before they moved. ('Up there they hit you all the time with a thing called a tawse . . .') Mr Grant did keep a belt in his desk, but Philip hadn't seen it yet. The teachers made a point of talking to him about England and describing their own visits there. As for him he had learned to call his satchel a school-bag, and had mystified his mother by asking for a play piece. 'Something to eat at morning break,' he had explained.

Gordon Downie and Neil Stuart were in Mr Grant's class with Philip; so were Robert Lachlan and Alastair Macdonald. Malcolm Drummond and James Stuart were in the class below. Also in Philip's class was the solitary boy he had noticed by the shops on his first day in Glasgow. His name was Thomas Fearn. He was solitary at school as well, and scorned by Gordon and his friends. He made Philip feel lucky; he could easily imagine being in the same position himself if Gordon hadn't adopted him.

He reached his own close. A grey-haired woman in a grey overall was washing the steps. She came every week; Mrs Macleod and his mother took it in turns to pay her and provide a bucket of whitening.

'The last lady who lived in your flat used to get the cobwebs down with a broom,' Mrs Macleod had said, looking at the corners above the two front doors. 'I'm afraid of spiders myself.'

'So am I,' Philip's mother had replied.

Philip didn't stay long indoors. He put his satchel away, ate a banana, and said he thought he would go for a walk.

'Where?' asked his mother.

'Just along by the canal.'

'Don't do anything silly.'

'No,' he said automatically. His mother didn't really expect him to do anything silly. She would have been surprised if she had seen him swinging by his arms over the water the other day.

Outside Martha was playing with Alison and Joan. They also wanted to know where he was going, and said they would come too.

'You'd better ask your mothers,' said Philip with resignation. Joan trotted obediently into the close; Alison stood where she was and bellowed: 'MUM!'

A window opened above their heads.

'Can I go for a walk with Martha and Philip?'

Mrs Downie gave him a swift glance and seemed satisfied. 'Yes all right,' she said, 'if you behave yourself and do what Philip tells you.'

Joan came back, buttoned into a neat little coat with a fur collar. 'I haven't to be late for tea,' she whispered, and gave him her hand so trustingly he felt he had no choice but to hold it.

As they turned the corner at the end of the road Philip saw

32

James and Neil ahead of them, sitting kicking their heels on the wall. He crossed to the other side, glad they weren't guarding the way he wanted to go. They might have been, because it was the gang's territory.

They saw him. 'Look, he's taking the wee ones for a walk!' said Neil, and they both laughed.

Philip felt Joan's hand quiver and defiantly kept hold of it.

'You be quiet, Neil Stuart!' said Alison. 'He's not taking us, we're going with him!'

'I don't like those boys,' said Martha.

'They're very naughty,' said Alison severely, 'and they ought to get a big smacking.'

'From their mummies?' asked Martha, delighted at the notion.

'From their daddies, and their teacher, and the policeman!'

Alison and Martha ran on ahead and presently Joan joined them, but Philip didn't relax until the first bend in the towpath had hidden the road from view. The curving canal reflected sky and bushes and three tall chimneys; by a trick of the ground at this point everything else had dropped out of sight. It was the rim of a world. Philip liked it along here when there was no Gordon exhorting him to daring deeds.

They passed the gap in the wall that led to the tunnel, and the hanging rope. Philip pointed neither out to the little girls. They were interested in climbing the bank a few yards further on, where a small gully led to the top. Philip went up behind them. They found a stretch of rough grass, all humps and hollows; Alison immediately appropriated the largest hollow as her house, and Joan and Martha also found houses. Philip sat down to wait until they got tired of this game. A little way away, by a row of back gardens, some boys were shouting to a dog. Philip wondered idly if Gordon's territory was theirs also, and whether they too used the rope.

He eventually got his companions to resume the walk by

promising that they could come here on the way back if they wanted to. They were nearly at the place where the canal crossed the river; he hurried ahead and had a long look from the parapet. Turning to offer the view to Martha he saw them all standing on the edge of the canal, pointing and staring at something the other side.

'Look!' hissed Alison.

In the long grass lay a shabby grey-haired man. His mouth was open and there was greyish stubble on his chin. His eyes were closed, but as Philip watched he opened them and yawned, sitting up and scratching his head.

'Oh,' said Martha, disappointed, 'we thought he was dead.'

'He's only an old tramp,' said Alison, equally let down.

Philip wondered how the man had got on to the pathless side of the canal.

He lifted Martha so that she could see the river, and then had to do the same for Alison. Both were heavy; Alison must be densely made. Today there was hardly anyone playing on the slope beneath the tower flats.

'What about you?' he asked Joan. She held out her arms without replying. He braced himself a third time, but she came up like a paper child, and in his surprise he nearly lifted her too far.

'There's the iver,' she murmured. She didn't say her r's.

At the far end of the bridge was a place where the wall could be climbed, and a path that led down the slope. Philip had been down with Gordon and the other boys, but he thought it would be too much of a scramble for the little girls. They went on to the lock, the first of a set of three by which the canal climbed to the level of the Ladyhill road.

If there was rubbish in this lock it didn't show. The water was deep and dark, with a thick scummy froth from the fall at the top end. Philip thought it looked like Guinness.

Some of the tenements ahead were being demolished. Philip couldn't quite see why; they looked just the same as those still standing all along the Ladyhill road. They were older than the ones in Hilton Avenue, decorated with domes and curlicues instead of being totally plain.

The sight of the road drawing near made Martha think of sweet shops.

'Sweeties!' said Alison, and they began jumping up and down on the stony path.

Philip hadn't any money, but they produced a penny each and hurried purposefully forward. The canal, level again, was now running alongside the road, and Philip looked ahead for some way of getting off the towpath. There was none; the road on the far side of the water dropped lower and lower until at last the canal crossed right over it. The bridge was disappointing, with a solid iron parapet higher than Philip's head, and Alison and Martha began to grizzle about aching legs.

'Come on,' said Philip, 'if we turn round now we'll soon be home.' He didn't really think they would; they had come a long way in the last few minutes, spurred on by the prospect of sweets. They were so upset at not getting any that when Philip noticed a way into a back street near the tower flats he took it in the hopes of finding a shop. He left the little girls waiting on the towpath; the path, which ran between the wall and the back of a hoarding, was slippery with black mud and impeded by a length of barbed wire and several lumps of concrete.

There was a shop, its window covered by a strong mesh shutter; Philip thought it was closed until he saw the open door. Inside a friendly Pakistani was serving a young woman whose baby sat on the counter next to a pile of tinned baked beans. Philip spent the two pennies and hurried back across the littered pavement. There was another lump of concrete in the middle of the road. Passing grimy entrances, he no longer wondered why tenements like these should be knocked down.

The sweets he had chosen lasted the children a good part of the way home. There were no more dragging feet. Martha picked flowers and Joan walked next to Philip and told him something at great length. Her voice was so quiet he only caught half the words, particularly when the others talked at the same time, but he looked as intelligent as he could and made interested noises.

'Oh look,' said Martha, 'a mouse.'

'It's a dead one,' said Alison.

'It's got nice soft fur,' said Martha, carefully picking it up. 'But its feet are cold and scrabbly.'

'Throw it away!' urged Philip.

'No, give it to me,' said Alison, snatching a dock leaf to hold it in. 'There, now we can take it home.'

'I suppose you could bury it in the garden . . .' said Philip doubtfully.

'Yes, let's,' they said.

Engrossed in it as they were they passed the place where they had played houses at the top of the bank without remembering Philip's promise. He didn't remind them.

James and Neil had gone from the bridge. There was nobody around when they reached home except the Macleods, just getting out of their car.

'Hallo, children,' beamed Mrs Macleod. Mr Macleod gave them a stiff little nod.

'Hallo,' said Philip.

'Look what we've got!' cried Martha.

'What – *oh* take it away, horrid thing,' said Mrs Macleod, peering into Alison's outstretched hands and recoiling fast.

'We're going to bury it,' they told her.

'Going to make it a nice little grave, are you?' Her smile

was rather strained. 'And did you pick some flowers to put on top?'

'No,' said Martha in what Philip called her pudding voice. 'These are for Alison's mummy.'

'Och well, that's – that's very nice,' said Mrs Macleod, and hurried inside.

They got the grave finished before tea. Martha told her mother about it.

'Really, Philip, couldn't you have stopped them?' she said, and sent Martha to wash her hands.

The sky was blue, with many-coloured clouds. The refuse incineration plant glowed pink. Philip pressed his face against the window and craned sideways to see the vivid sunset behind the black fretwork struts of the gasometer. His breath made a smeary pattern on the glass. 'Now look what you've done,' said his mother.

'This is a good sky window,' said Philip.

Gordon came for him after tea. He slipped away quickly while his mother was still thinking it was one of the little girls, and telling Martha she couldn't play out any more today.

Gordon had the others with him. They walked down the road talking and laughing. Philip was on the end of the line where he couldn't always hear what was being said, but he joined in all the laughter. They passed a close with a bicycle at the foot of the stairs and James slipped inside; when he caught them up a moment later he had two valves to show.

They came to another front path with three bicycles leaning against the fence.

'Go on, Philip,' said Gordon, 'see how many you can get.'

'Me?'

'Yes, you.' Gordon gave him an encouraging grin, and then they all went on and left him to it. He stood wretched and undecided, watching their backs in the deserted street. He even thought of going home, until Gordon turned his head; then he made a quick dash at the first bike and fumbled with wet hands round its front wheel.

He had got three when he fled because he heard a car coming. The others were waiting further along.

'Not bad,' said Gordon.

'I can get six there,' snorted James.

'Philip's a beginner yet.'

They reached the shops and bought chips. Lights were on in the launderette and patient figures sat in the window. They went inside, and the attendant watched their greasy fingers as they prowled round the machines in single file and left by the other door.

'Made them all feel hungry,' said Gordon with satisfaction, and clambered on to the top of the pillar box. Robert tried the drawers of the cigarette machine to see if it was out of order. James and Neil went to press button B in the telephone kiosk and left a bundle of fragrant chip wrappings on the directory shelf.

It was growing dark when they started home. Philip felt the valves in his pocket; Gordon had let him keep them. As he passed the place where the three bikes still leaned against the fence he hung back a little and dropped the valves quietly in the gravel.

The others had found a tin can and were sending it up the road. Philip took his place on the end of the line and managed an occasional kick. It made a beautiful noise.

Five

It was raining. Philip stood in the school playground, hands in pockets, and wondered how bad the weather would have to be before it was considered too bad for them to go outside at break. He supposed he would find out in winter.

Actually he could have been under cover if he had wanted. There was room beneath the arch, in the wide tunnel which cut through the building; presumably for this very purpose, as it even had a seat inside it. Most of the girls were there, but not many of the boys.

Gordon had chosen to be in the wettest place of all, where water splashed from a broken drainpipe on to the asphalt. A length of new guttering leaned against the wall, left by the workmen who were in the middle of repairs. (They at least considered it too wet to be outside today.) Gordon picked it up and used it to catch and direct the stream. One of the places he decided to send it was down the neck of Thomas Fearn, who was standing with his back turned nearby.

Thomas Fearn often stood alone in the playground, staring ahead in an unseeing way as though he was busy thinking.

At the impact of the water he jumped violently and shook himself. Although Philip shivered in sympathy he couldn't help laughing.

'Drowned rat!' said Neil.

Thomas mopped himself with a handkerchief and seemed not to hear. He made Philip uncomfortable; he often did. They were too alike for comfort. Thomas chose to be solitary, and Philip knew he would have done the same if Gordon hadn't taken him up. Sometimes, breathless from Gordon's rough jollying, he even envied Thomas his proud aloof state; he felt he himself was nothing but a plaything to Gordon, an English joke, picked out by the accident of his voice. But at times like these he was guiltily glad not to be Thomas. He fingered the dry handkerchief in his own pocket and wondered if he dared offer it to the drowned rat.

'Did you see that, Philip?' Gordon asked him.

'Yes.' He grinned nervously.

Thomas Fearn walked away.

'Why is everyone so nasty to him?' asked Philip.

'Don't you know?' said Gordon. 'He's a clipe.'

'A clipe?'

'He sneaks to the teachers – tells tales.'

'O-oh.' Philip was relieved, yet disappointed. At least he needn't feel sorry for Thomas any more.

The rain stopped after lunch. At four o'clock the playground was dry and the men were working again on the drainpipes and gutters. They had a ladder.

'Easy way on to the roof,' said James.

'Not with them around,' said Gordon.

'If they left it there.'

'They wouldn't,' said Gordon regretfully.

'They do while they have their break. They have it when we have ours; I noticed yesterday,' said Philip.

'Good for you,' said Gordon. 'We could go up.'

'We could climb the tower with old Mac's hat and umbrella,' said James.

'What for?' asked Philip blankly. Mac was the headmaster, Mr Macpherson. The tower was in the middle of the roof.

'Oh, you don't know anything.'

'Somebody once did it,' said Gordon. 'He put old Mac's hat on top of the weathervane, and hung his umbrella on one of the arms.'

'Philip could do that,' said Neil maliciously.

'I bet he could too,' said Gordon. 'Couldn't you, Philip?'

He tried to turn it into a joke. 'Not carrying an umbrella.'

'It's a help, the umbrella. You hook it on things and pull yourself up. And you could wear the hat.'

'I don't know where he keeps them.'

'On the pegs outside his door,' said several voices together.

'I dare you,' said Gordon. 'Go on, Philip. You'll be famous.'

'I'd get the belt,' said Philip.

'The other boy didn't,' they assured him. 'Old Mac didn't do anything to him at all.'

'Perhaps he didn't know who it was.'

'Och, yes, everyone knew. Like I said, he was famous. What was his name? Holden. John Holden.'

'I don't think I want to be famous.'

'He daren't,' said James.

'You're wasting your time,' agreed Neil. 'He'll never do it.'

'You will, won't you, Philip? Come on now,' urged Gordon, fixing him with his eye, 'say you will.'

'Perhaps the ladder won't be there tomorrow.'

James laughed.

'If it isn't it can't be helped,' said Gordon. 'But if it is, then you will. Won't you?'

'Careful!' said somebody. 'Thomas Fearn!'

A silence fell as Thomas Fearn passed. They all watched until he was out of earshot.

'That's settled then,' said Gordon.

'I never said . . .' protested Philip.

'Only if the ladder's there, of course. The ladder makes it easy. John Holden didn't have a ladder, but we'll let you.'

'But . . .' said Philip.

'That's the boy!' said Gordon, and gave him an encouraging whack across the shoulders. And Philip knew it was no good; if the ladder was there tomorrow he would have to climb it. After that heaven knew what would happen; he couldn't see himself managing to ascend the slope of the roof and then the tower, even with an umbrella to hook on things. In the depths of his stomach he felt sure he would fall. But he knew he would have to try.

Today he didn't go out after he got home from school. He sat in his place at the empty table and watched dust lorries in ones and twos grinding up the road across the valley.

'I'm not getting tea yet,' said his mother.

'No.'

'I suppose you're hungry?'

Philip considered. 'I wouldn't mind some bread and butter,' he said.

'Perhaps you wouldn't mind getting it either.'

'All right,' agreed Philip. He had just taken the bread out when Martha came to the door.

'This is me in for a biscuit,' she said. Her voice already had a distinctly Scottish flavour. 'And I want one for Alison and one for Joan.'

Philip changed his mind and decided he would have a biscuit too. He ate it standing by the kitchen window. It was the same view as from the living-room, but the height of the sill cut off the lower part and concentrated his attention on the skyline. The hill behind the refuse incineration plant had a fuzzy crown of trees; Mrs Macleod had told them it was the edge of a park.

'Philip, just look at the crumbs you've made,' said his

42

mother. 'At least Martha eats her biscuits in the garden. And if you don't want the bread why are you leaving it out to get stale?'

'Sorry.' He put it away. Then, since his mother was already sweeping up his crumbs herself, he offered to empty some waste paper baskets. The dustbins were in the farthest corner of the back garden, down sixteen steps and along a path, so she sounded quite mollified as she accepted.

He met the little girls in the close.

'We've been to see how the mouse was getting on,' said Martha.

'You don't mean you dug it up?'

'We didn't move it,' said Alison. 'We just had a look.'

'I hope you put the earth back.'

'Yes, and then we put some leaves because its legs still showed.'

Philip wondered uneasily how deep they had made the original grave.

Mrs Macleod was pegging out washing.

'Helping your mother?'

'Yes,' said Philip, since he could scarcely say less.

'That's right. It's nice to see a boy who's not afraid to give a hand.'

'I help Mummy too,' said Martha. 'I help her put the washing on the line.' She looked at the basket of damp clothes standing on the grass.

'Well,' said Mrs Macleod brightly. 'Well,' she continued on a more wavering note, having glanced at Martha's hands, 'yes, that's – that must be nice too. I haven't any children to help me, but I'm used to managing.'

'You could get a dog,' said Martha.

'Oh, we did have one once.'

'Why haven't you still? Where's it gone?'

'He was taken not well, you see.'

43

'Did he die?'

'Martha, stop asking questions,' muttered Philip.

'Och, they're all the same at that age. Yes, he died.'

'Did you bury him in the garden?'

'Gracious me, no. I think Tom took him somewhere along by the canal; that's what people usually do.' She pointed vaguely.

Martha had stopped listening. She was looking up at the windows of their flat. 'I can see Daddy,' she said.

'Call to him,' said Alison. 'MISTER GRAY!'

He opened the window and leaned out. 'Hallo, Alison!' he said. 'Hallo, Martha! Hallo, Joan!'

Joan coloured and started to go home.

'Evening, Mrs Macleod. Hallo, Philip.'

He was early. Philip thought it might not be a good idea to rush in straight away expecting tea. But his mother called them up quite soon; his father's arrival must have put her into a bustling mood, which was handy. If not brisk at this time of day she tended to be very much the opposite, wandering from room to room considering jobs that needed to be done and answering any remark of Martha's with the command to be quiet and let her think.

In Grantham, Philip remembered, this would have been his father's usual time for coming home. In Grantham he had never gone to the office on a Saturday either. Before the move he had said how lucky he was to get the Glasgow promotion; he hadn't mentioned anything about having to work harder.

Perhaps Philip's father was also thinking about those days, because when tea was over he asked Philip if he would like to come for a walk, which was something they had often done in Grantham.

'Me too!' said Martha, grizzling already in anticipation of her mother's reply. 'I never get to go out after tea!'

'You can't go with Daddy, but if you like – Martha, will

44

you stop that noise and listen to me? *Listen!* – if you like, as we're earlier today, you can just play outside while I get your bath ready. Only you must promise to come in the minute I call.'

'Yes,' said Martha tearfully.

As they left her behind and started up the road they were overtaken by the gang.

'Hallo, Gordon!' said Mr Gray. He was good at remembering people's names. Philip smiled shyly, liking to be seen with his father.

'Hallo,' said Gordon, his voice very Scottish and aloof.

When the two of them reached the corner Philip asked: 'Which way shall we go?'

'Where would you like to go?' said his father.

'Along by the canal?' The gang were heading straight on, across the valley and up the hill.

'Right, you lead. You've had more chance to explore than me; I expect you know all the best walks.'

Philip turned right, into the gang's territory; the burial ground (according to Mrs Macleod) for all dogs round about.

'This,' he said, and broke off to think of the right word, 'this is a curious place.'

'Curious, is it?' His father kept a serious mouth, but his eyes wrinkled.

'Nothing is quite where you'd expect it to be. If you try to draw a map with everything on, the canal and the river and the roads and the railway, there's always something that doesn't fit.'

'Have you looked on our big map of Glasgow?'

'No . . .' He felt that would be a dull and cheating thing to do, but he didn't know how to explain to his father. He pointed to the wall by the towpath and said: 'There used to be a railway over there. It goes all along the bottom of the gardens in our road.'

'Yes, it's rather a pity they closed that line. I expect it was quite convenient.'

'There's where it goes into a tunnel.'

'Does it?' His father sprang agilely over the broken wall and followed the path down the grass bank, but stopped short of dropping on to the track. They stood for a moment and heard water drip inside the black mouth below.

'Not even blocked off,' marvelled his father.

'It is further along.'

'Why, have you been in?'

'Gordon – no, I think it was one of the others – Robert – said it was.'

'Well!' said his father and went bounding back to the towpath.

'There's the Ladyhill road over there.' Philip pointed to the distant line of tenements.

His father didn't hear. 'Good heavens, that's dangerous!' He had noticed the swinging rope.

'Mm,' said Philip.

'It must go right out over the canal . . . and the ground's been worn quite smooth on the bank.'

'Yes.' On a sudden impulse Philip said: 'I went a little way into the old tunnel. We all did. It was creepy.'

'I'm not surprised. Did you have any light?'

'A match. It went out.'

'Rrrrr!' His father shuddered. 'Did you run?'

'Yes!'

Philip edged ahead, trying to draw his father along more quickly, until they reached the place where the towpath was bounded by the parapet and he could say: 'Look over here.'

His father was satisfactorily impressed by the river.

'Would you like to go down?' asked Philip. 'There's a way over the wall.'

'Fine.'

They climbed over the wall on to the green slope below the tower flats. A path zigzagged to the bottom. The far bank of the river was thickly wooded, and a large black hole showed through the foliage.

'The other end of the old tunnel,' said Philip. 'And then it must have crossed the river.' Three stone-built piers stood out of the rushing water in a slanting line, rather dwarfed by the canal bridge beside them. It had two great arches; one for the river and one for another branch of the disused railway which had apparently run along the river bank. Deep weed-fringed sockets showed where sleepers had been torn out of the ground, and a cracked mossy platform suggested a one-time station. Philip and his father walked through the second arch. It glistened darkly above their heads and occasional drips fell.

'The canal is coming through,' said Philip.

'The stones must be saturated.'

'Will it all leak away in the end, do you think?'

'That, or dry from on top perhaps. But I think canals last a good while even when they're not used.'

On the other side of the arch they came to a stretch of river which was invisible from the towpath. Here the valley was flattened, and their view was bounded by the line of the canal bank behind, and another, lower bridge in front, hiding the further reaches of the river. A stone wall ran to the bridge and became its parapet; in the wall was an open gateway, with a slope leading up to it. On the far side of the gateway they found a road. Philip knew what road it must be; they had driven along it a couple of times: it cut across from the Ladyhill road and came out at GORDON DOWNIE OK. He even recognised, now that he was on top of it, the narrow river bridge where every car had to brake to a crawl.

'This must be how people got to that old station, if there was one. I expect that gateway was the way in,' said Philip.

He had previously imagined them scrambling down the slope from the canal.

'And I imagine if we go up here it'll take us home,' said his father, looking rather pleased to have a pavement under his feet again.

'Yes,' said Philip, himself a bit disappointed; he hadn't supposed civilisation was so close.

The road made one of the sharp twists that Philip had come to expect in this place and ran uphill. On one side, behind high walls, was the modern gasworks; on the other a row of cottages huddled in the shadow of the canal bank. As they left the bridge a woman crossed from the cottages carrying a bowl of milk and an open tin of cat food. She set them down on the end of the parapet and called. Immediately five cats appeared, snaking one after the other round the end of the gasworks wall.

Mr Gray watched with interest and said: 'I bet they're grateful for that.'

'Yes, they come every day.' The woman wore slippers and a stained overall; her hair was so red Philip knew it must be dyed. 'I think they're left, you know, from the railway. I don't grudge them a bit of food. They keep the rats down.'

Philip ran a finger along the back of one small striped cat. Though wild and bony it had not forgotten how to purr.

'I wouldn't live there for a million pounds,' said Mr Gray as they left the last cottage behind. 'Rats and damp!'

'Wouldn't you?' Philip thought the cottages looked rather attractive; a change from the endless flats.

Just as they reached the corner of their own road they heard a loud ringing, and a fire engine went past. It crossed the valley and laboured up the hill. Thick black smoke rose from a point behind the horizon.

'Looks like old motor tyres in that lot,' said Mr Gray. 'I wonder where it is.'

'In the tar distillery,' guessed Philip. He remembered Gordon saying how the gang sometimes set fire to piles of rubbish in the deserted part of the factory.

Another fire engine approached. Philip wondered if anyone would get caught. He hoped they all would, and then there would be nobody to make him climb the school tower to-morrow. But he didn't think it likely. They had lit fires before and knew the right tricks.

'How are you settling down at school?' asked his father, just as though he could read his mind.

Philip jumped. 'Oh, all right,' he said vaguely.

'Is it very different from England?'

'Not really. Little things. They don't have a teacher on playground duty.' Now why had he mentioned that, when he knew he must keep off the subject of the playground?

'Never? How do they stop the fights?'

'Plenty of people fought at my other school.' (Though nobody had actually climbed the roof.) 'I don't know; perhaps they watch us through the window.' (Perhaps somebody would come rushing out: 'Philip Gray, get off that ladder. I'll give you the belt.' He still hadn't had the belt, though he had seen it used on another boy.)

They reached their close. 'There's something I want to look at,' he remembered, scanning the front garden.

'What?'

'A mouse's grave. That must be it.'

The mouse lay under some wilting leaves. It looked very dead indeed by this time. Philip's father scooped it up on a plastic spade left by the children, took it down the back steps and hurled it over the fence into the old railway cutting.

'Better not tell Mummy,' he said.

Six

Next morning Philip ate his breakfast with little appetite, and looked at the weather. Rain was falling, pricking the window in slanting lines. If it continued all morning the men wouldn't work on the roof and their ladder wouldn't be there. But he was afraid it was going to stop. Although the sky was grey, a strange light seemed to come from inside things; a sort of bursting brightness. The greenery was so green it hurt.

'. . . and if a wolf got into this house – ' Martha was saying.

'There are no wolves in England – in Britain,' said Mrs Gray. She was cross this morning because of the smell from the tar distillery. All the windows were closed, but still it was seeping in; a damp black smell with a flavour of mothballs and soot. 'Eat up, Philip,' she said.

'I've finished,' said Philip, whose throat felt unnaturally small.

'You haven't.'

'I mean I don't want any more.'

His mother stared. 'You'll never get through the morning on that,' she said.

'I feel full.'

'Is Britain in Glasgow?' asked Martha, but nobody answered.

'Can't you at least eat what's on your plate? It's such a waste!'

'I don't think I can,' said Philip apologetically.

'Then you might as well let me give you a lift,' said his father, getting up from the table. 'Keep you dry.'

Philip was able to put on his blazer in a great hurry and leave without further ado. His father usually went before he did. As they walked out to the car neither commented on the fact that the rain had almost stopped. The tar smell was very strong in the close.

The wet road shone. 'Have a good day,' said Philip's father; and Philip found himself set down in the empty playground at twenty to nine with a bad day ahead of him. He had avoided breakfast, and the company of the gang on the way to school, but he would not be able to avoid anything else.

The rain stopped. The men brought out their ladder and started work. The playground filled, and the gang arrived to surround Philip and nudge him in the ribs, with many significant glances at the tower.

'Gordon,' said Philip in a low voice. He wanted to say he wouldn't do it.

'We're counting on you,' said Gordon.

The bell rang. They all went in to their classrooms.

'Gordon Downie,' said Mr Grant. He sounded angry; Philip wondered if he had found out who had started the fire the evening before. Not that that was really anything to do with the school.

'Yes, sir?' said Gordon.

'There's talk,' said Mr Grant, 'of people climbing the school roof. And you're behind it. Don't try to say anything, just listen to me. If anyone climbs that roof, I shall give you the belt. Do you understand?'

'Yes, sir.' Gordon's face was red, but he met Mr Grant's

eyes. Several other people were looking at Thomas Fearn, who had his head bent and seemed not to notice.

'Remember it then,' said Mr Grant curtly.

As soon as Gordon's eyes were free he turned them on Thomas Fearn. His colour was mostly due to anger, Philip saw. Thomas must have felt the intensity of his stare; he returned it for a moment, and Gordon's lips formed a single spitting word. 'Clipe,' it might have been, or 'traitor!'

Philip had since yesterday become so used to the idea that he couldn't escape the climb that at first he simply considered Gordon's future belting as an inevitable by-product of his own ordeal. Gradually he realised that Gordon's wishes were bound to be changed by Mr Grant's threat. He felt a rush of relief; and when it began to die down he thought of Thomas Fearn with uneasy wonder.

At break he discovered most of the gang were sorry for him. 'Never mind,' they said, 'it wasn't your fault.' As soon as the story had been passed on to those members who weren't in Mr Grant's class, the gang converged on Thomas Fearn. He got his back against the wall when he saw them coming, and his face looked tight.

'Who's a clipe?' they cried.

'I'm not afraid of hard names,' said Thomas.

'You're not denying it then?'

'Somebody had to put a stop to you.'

'Somebody did, did they? That's what you think, is it?' Gordon was pointing his finger at Thomas as he spoke, and drawing nearer, so that he ended up jabbing him in the chest. 'Right, if you're not afraid of hard names you can just tell us what you are. Say *I'm a clipe*. Say it, come on, come on!'

Thomas blinked and swallowed. Then James and Neil took an ankle each, and pulled; and he went down on the ground with the gang on top of him.

Philip thought he wouldn't look. Then he couldn't help it.

Thomas was on his back, and kept trying to curl into a ball, but they wouldn't let him. His face was twisted and he hissed through his teeth.

'Stop it!' exclaimed Philip. 'Stop it, stop it! Here comes Mr Grant!'

The heap of boys rolled apart. The gang sprang to their feet and looked around. Thomas got rather more slowly to his. Mr Grant was not coming. The workmen were, however; they had finished their tea break early. Their foreman was huge and burly, and he shot an ugly glance at the gang. Whether it was just general dislike of boys or whether he knew they had recently had designs on his ladder, nobody waited to find out.

Philip and Thomas were the last to walk away.

'Are you all right?' asked Philip.

'Yes,' said Thomas dourly.

'It was – er – well – thank you for – '

'Nobody but a fool would climb that tower,' said Thomas.

'I suppose not . . .'

'And you looked a proper fool to me.'

Philip was too deadened by recent events to find an answer to this.

'But there,' said Thomas, 'you don't know what happened to the other.'

'Gordon said he didn't get the belt or anything. He was famous.'

'He was famous right enough, if that's what you wanted.'

'I didn't,' said Philip indignantly.

'He broke his thigh.'

'*Oh*,' said Philip. 'That was why you – well – thank you.'

'You already thanked me once. Your friends are wanting you.'

Philip wasn't sure that he wanted them; or that they had ever been his friends. But it turned out they didn't want him either, or at least not in any friendly sense.

'You should have stayed together,' said James. 'You make a nice pair.'

'You taking care of him, and him taking care of you – och yes!' said Gordon. 'It brings the tears to my eyes.'

'You were seven to one,' muttered Philip. 'It wasn't fair.'

'Oh dear, it wasn't fair,' said Neil in an attempt at an English voice.

'He asked for it,' said Gordon.

'He knew if I climbed up there I'd probably have a bad fall,' Philip stammered a little, hearing Thomas's voice in his head: *And you looked a proper fool to me.* 'You never told me about the other boy falling.'

'You never asked,' said Gordon.

'He thinks it *wasn't fair*,' said Neil.

'Don't keep on at him,' said Robert.

'No we'd better not,' agreed James. 'After all it's seven to one, and he might cry.'

'If he does we'll give him something to cry about,' said Neil.

'No we won't,' said Gordon in tones of authority. 'He's not worth bothering with.'

They all went away and left Philip by himself. His eyes were as dry as anyone could wish, but he felt grey inside.

During the next few days he found out how much they bothered with him. There were occasional taunts in the playground and linking of his name with Thomas Fearn's, though Thomas was as aloof as ever and never spoke to him. There was one time when he was going down the road and met the gang coming the other way; he hoped he would be ignored, but instead they closed round him and he felt their hands pulling out pockets and tweaking buttons, crumpling his collar and flicking his tie. A moment later they had passed on, leaving him thoroughly tousled.

His bicycle valves went. As soon as it happened he realised

he should have expected it. This time he accepted his father's offer of replacements from the cycle shop near his office, and cautiously suggested that his father might buy half a dozen so as to provide some spares. He asked if he could keep his bicycle inside the house, but was not really surprised when his mother said no.

'We've scarcely room to move as it is. You'd better put it out at the back.'

He leaned it against the wall between a bunker and a bath full of coal. There was no shelter, and the sixteen steps would be a nuisance when he wanted to use it. The next day the valves were gone again.

His mother said it was quite ridiculous. His father agreed it was a bit much. Philip transferred the bike to its old place, kept the next pair of valves inside the house, and hoped being flat most of the time wouldn't have a bad effect on the tyres.

That Sunday they all went for a walk.

'We'll show Mummy your place, shall we, Philip?' said his father.

'Where's this?' asked his mother.

'Oh, along the canal to the right here and all the open ground across to the Ladyhill road. Am I right, Philip?'

He nodded.

'I'd hardly call that a place,' said his mother.

'Well, Philip does, and he knows it.'

'I don't know it very well,' said Philip as they turned off along the towpath. 'It's too big.'

'I know it,' said Martha. 'There's a car in the water and mattresses and things.'

'No,' said Philip, 'that's the other way.'

'Those are your landmarks, I suppose,' said their mother with a resigned smile. But she seemed prepared to enjoy herself, looking about her as they walked along and commenting on the wild flowers. Philip was glad when they passed another family in what were obviously their best clothes; he thought it would encourage his mother to think this a suitable direction for a Sunday stroll.

After she had seen the river, and Martha had been lifted up to look too, Philip said: 'We needn't go any further beside the canal if you don't want to. We could turn off along that path we just passed.'

It was something he had not yet explored; the rutted sunken track that left the towpath just before the bridge and followed the course of the river, though high above it. The choice proved a good one; before they had gone more than a few yards in the shade of the great beeches, his mother said in tones of pleased surprise: 'Now this is nice!'

'Yes, it is,' said his father.

Philip said: 'The old tunnel comes out just about here. We might be right over it now.' He hopped up on to the crown of the bank and surveyed the steep fall of wooded ground down to the river. The river itself scarcely showed through the branches of the trees. 'I expect that's it.' He indicated to his father a jutting line of mossy stones set across the hill. The ground was thickly covered in ivy, which made it easy for Philip to scramble down and see; his father stayed behind to prevent Martha from following, while his mother went slowly on along the path. The stones were indeed the top of the arch, but Philip couldn't get any further because the ground took a steeper plunge and became almost sheer.

'What a pity,' he said. 'I've seen inside it from the other end, and I'd like to have seen it from this.'

They rejoined his mother and went on, Philip and Martha keeping to the top of the bank where an extra path had been worn. Presently they saw through the trees a small building at the water's edge. It had a hole in the roof and looked like some kind of derelict mill; there was a weir, and a narrow channel leading the water to an arch in the wall of the building.

Here it was easier to climb down, and everyone except Mrs Gray did so, but they found chainlink fencing had been erected to stop explorers reaching the mill. Philip thought they might work their way round it until they came to the water's edge, and then follow the bank upstream to the tunnel mouth; but they soon came to an impenetrable clump of thorn bushes.

'Ah well,' said his father, 'even if we could have got inside we've no torch, and matches don't give a very satisfactory light.'

'Don't let Martha tear her coat,' called Mrs Gray.

'It's all right, we're coming back up now.'

A little further on the path left the river and wound through a small wilderness and past some reservoirs, coming out suddenly in a residential street.

'Where are we, I wonder?' said Mr Gray. 'Oh yes, I know. I've driven along here. The Ladyhill road's that way, and we want to go up here.'

'These are rather nice houses,' said Mrs Gray. They were stone, semi-detached with flourishing front gardens. Philip was reminded a little of the street they had lived in in Grantham.

'Like to buy one?' asked Mr Gray, half joking.

'Well, there might be a lot to be said for it,' she answered seriously. 'We can't stay in the flat for ever, even if we liked it.'

'I thought you'd want to go further.'

'So did I, but this all seems so pleasant . . . Look,' (they were passing a row of shops) 'there's a post office, and even a bank.'

'And I expect from round here Philip could still go to the same school.'

Philip was on in front, so his unenthusiastic face aroused no comment. He didn't want to think about school on a Sunday; and he didn't particularly want to think about moving either.

Seven

Philip sat doodling by the window. He had been trying to draw a map of the place and had, as usual, given it up in disgust. He hadn't been there since the family walk a week or two earlier, for fear of meeting the gang. On that occasion he had felt protected by his parents. Though in fact the gang didn't go there all that often; he was watching them at this moment making their way along the towpath in the opposite direction. They were kicking something; he could hear the laughter. When they got as far as the sawmill they would very likely make one of the huge planks into a seesaw. They had done it once before when Philip was with them; working together they had just been able to shift it. He wished he was with them now.

He sometimes thought it might have been better if he'd been allowed to climb the roof and fall off. Gordon would surely have felt repentant if Philip had broken his leg. Philip would have refused to betray anyone; despite earnest questioning by the teachers he would insist that it had been entirely his own idea. 'He's a plucky little chap,' Gordon would tell the gang; and, standing by Philip's hospital bed: 'I say, young 'un, do you think you can ever forgive me?' (In Philip's mind the broken leg had become a permanent injury.) 'Of course, Gordon,' he would murmur faintly. 'I already have. Oh Gordon, don't cry.' (It was his deathbed now.)

But of course Gordon would never talk like that. Thomas Fearn's words on hearing of the tragedy were easier to imagine. 'I thought he looked a proper fool,' said the voice of Thomas. The fantasy shattered.

Down in the garden Martha and Alison were quarrelling.

'I'll be mother and you can be my babies.'

'No, I'll be mother.'

'No, *I* want to be mother – '

'No, *I* – '

'I! I! I!' shouted Martha.

The split between Philip and Gordon hadn't affected the younger ones; Martha still saw just as much of Alison and Joan, the former of whom had been in trouble recently for scratching ALISON DOWNIE OK on her own front door. 'If I'd caught her at it I'd have given her a good hiding,' her mother had said. 'Since it was Jim she just had to cry and say she didn't mean to. Didn't mean to! Half an hour's solid work – it must have been. But Jim can't see anything round Alison. Believe me, Mrs Gray, she deserves an Oscar for some of the performances she's put on for him.'

Martha and Alison were making Joan a bed on the grass. 'I canny get it right,' complained Martha.

'Not *canny*. *Can't*,' said Alison. 'You should know that.'

Joan seemed uncertain which was her parent. 'Good night, mummies,' she said submissively.

Philip suddenly remembered that he had seen the gang heading away from their territory a little earlier. It was an opportunity to go there himself, and here he was sitting wasting it. He took an apple from the kitchen and set off at once.

The towpath was deserted. It was a warm breezy afternoon;

59

the hanging rope moved gently of its own accord, as though a ghost were swinging there. He strode along with unusual vigour, feeling glad to be out.

He thought he would take the track beside the river and have another look at the old mill. They had found it impossible to reach the upstream end of the chainlink fencing, but they hadn't tried the downstream end. He discovered now that he could get to it fairly easily. The last post was stuck in at the point where the bank shelved steeply to the river two feet below, and a tangle of barbed wire had been added beyond it. Philip saw that if it weren't for the barbed wire he would be able to swing himself round the post. Gingerly he took hold of the topmost loop and pulled. With a scraping sound the end came free.

It took him quite a while to finish the job. There was just the one strand, but sometimes it was hard to see where to pull next; it was like undoing a giant knot. Flakes of rust fell round his feet. At last the other end left the post, and the wire dropped into the river.

Getting round the post was easy, and the mill was just a few yards away. He went up a flight of steps and found a door with a broken lock which led into a little room. There was a square hole in the floor with the murmur of water under it, and a ragged hole in the roof with dusty sunlight streaming through. The one glassless window faced the river. It was a perfect place; nobody could possibly know he was there.

His hands were sore from grasping the wire. He rubbed them down the sides of his trousers as he gazed through the hole in the floor at the unmoving rusty machinery beneath. He had one or two scratches; nothing much.

There were a couple of sun-warmed sacks to sit on. The hessian smell tickled Philip's nose and reminded him of hay lofts. He took the apple out of his pocket and ate it slowly, wondering how long it was since anybody else had been in here. There was a cigarette packet amid the scattering of dead leaves on the floor; perhaps people had come quite a lot before the fence was put up. He threw the packet and his core into the river together, leaning out of the window to watch them float away. The sound of the weir drowned the smaller sound of water under the floor. He could see the children from the tower flats playing on the far green slope. They seemed very remote.

He went to explore outside, and crouched on the smooth ledge of concrete watching water flow darkly along the narrow channel which led it from the river into the mill. On the inside of the fence the undergrowth was even thicker, and the only place clear enough to walk was a pebbly strip at the very edge of the river. He was delighted when this led him right past the other end of the fence and on upstream, until he eventually came level with the mouth of the tunnel. He scrambled up through the bushes and went in. He wanted to see how brave he was without the gang striking matches and chivvying him along. Not very brave, he discovered; once the daylight failed his nerve failed too. He thought it would have been better if he hadn't been told the tunnel was blocked; he might have dared to move on towards the promise of light at the other end, but to go into the blackness not knowing at what point it became solid . . . the idea made him shiver, and he hurried out in some disorder.

He glanced at his watch and saw that he ought to be going. He retraced his steps to the mill; no time for another look at the upper room, but he would come again. He would often come.

Tea was on the table when he got home.

'Oh there you are,' said his mother. 'Call Martha would you.'

Martha arrived empty-handed and was told to go back for the vast quantity of things which she had earlier considered necessary for their game.

'I'll get them after tea,' she said.

'You'll get them now,' said her mother.

After a little further argument Martha went, stumping up and down the steps in a martyred way with her arms dangling feebly at her sides.

'Don't be ridiculous, Martha,' said her mother as she came in to deposit one doll, 'you can carry more at a time than that.'

'Oh,' said Martha.

When she next arrived she had all the remaining toys piled up to her chin.

'And I can't find my teddy!' she said defiantly.

'Is he under the bed?' said her mother.

'No, I had him outside.'

'You shouldn't have done. You can't take him to bed with you if he's all dirty. Go and fetch him in at once.'

'He's not there.'

'Not where?' Her mother's voice grew sharper. 'You don't mean he's lost, do you? Whereabouts did you have him?'

'I don't know.'

'You must know. You come outside with me now, and show me where you were playing.' She whirled Martha away. Philip saw part of the search from the window, and heard the questioning of Alison and Joan. Martha's teddy had been a present from her parents; it was large and very furry. Philip hadn't then wanted to pass on his own hard balding bear, which even now he kept in a special place at the back of a drawer.

When they returned Martha's mother was saying: 'You must have left it out at the front, that's all, and somebody's stolen it. You know you've been told not to leave things there.'

She was too angry about the theft to give Martha any

sympathy, and Martha was too intimidated by the anger to expect any. Philip's father came in soon afterwards, and Mrs Gray ceased supervising their tea in order to rage at him as he took off his coat and sat down.

'First Philip's valves and now this! What kind of people would steal a child's teddy?'

'Perhaps Alison threw it over the fence?' he suggested. Once before when he was at home Alison had hurled a treasured plastic bottle of Martha's into the railway cutting, and he had had to climb over and search for it. As he climbed back Mrs Downie had come rushing out to give Alison a good smack 'not so much for throwing it', she had said, 'as for standing there watching Mr Gray on the fence as though it was a show put on for her benefit!'

But Martha didn't think Alison had thrown it anywhere.

'I'll have a look anyway,' he said, frowning with concern. 'It'll be an awful shame if it's really gone.'

'I want my teddy,' said Martha, suddenly beginning to cry. 'He had brown eyes, and he was so nice always!'

'Well, it's your own fault,' said her mother. 'You know perfectly well, Mrs Macleod's told you and I've told you, that if you leave things out at the front they get stolen. If you live in a place like this you've got to think of things like that.'

'Is he really stolen then?' said Martha breathlessly. 'Is he really?'

'Oh no, I don't suppose so. I expect we'll find him.'

Martha was not convinced by this abrupt change of front. 'He is! He is!' she roared.

Mrs Gray pulled Martha on to her lap and stifled some of the noise in a maternal hug, saying sharply over her head: 'Are you going to go and look down the cutting?' Now that Martha was so upset she seemed to have decided to blame the missing toy on her husband instead.

Philip quickly finished his tea and went out with his father, glad to escape from the fraught atmosphere inside the house. He said he would walk down the road to the first bend and look in the patch of waste ground; someone might have picked the teddy up while passing and dropped it again along there. He didn't say what kind of person he had in mind; at that stage he wasn't admitting it even to himself.

The waste ground was larger than he had thought. He pushed his way through the long rank grass finding tins and bottles, and decomposing piles of garden rubbish thrown over by the people who lived on either side. There was no sign of the teddy.

He walked slowly home and went into the back garden. He found his father by the fence brushing grass seeds off his trousers.

'It gets worse and worse in that cutting,' he said. 'Did you have any luck?'

'No,' said Philip.

'Nor me. Poor old Martha. It is tough.'

'Yes.'

'I suppose the more poverty there is in a place, the more dishonesty you'll get . . . not that this is by any means one of the poorest areas of Glasgow. Do you wish we didn't live here?'

Philip was startled by the question; he had thought his father was speaking chiefly to himself. Several pictures came into his head before he replied. The school playground; the view from the parapet where the canal crossed the river; Gordon and the gang; his father's face wearing an expression of cautious glee the day he had come home to their Grantham house and said to them, 'How would you like to move to Scotland?'

'No, I like it here,' said Philip.

'Do you?' Mr Gray looked pleased.

'And Martha likes having Alison and Joan.'

'Yes, we've got good neighbours . . . and when the weather gets warmer we must go for some outings in the car, there's lovely country within reach – you've made friends too, haven't you?'

Philip said nothing.

'Of course it's different at your age; you don't want to play outside all the time, and you get to know people at school who live further away.'

'Yes,' said Philip.

'Do you miss John Eccles much?'

'No,' said Philip, surprised to find it was so. John had written him one letter some weeks ago, and he had not yet replied. 'Well, sort of.'

'Mm,' said his father.

'There's a boy at school called Thomas Fearn – ' said Philip quickly. 'He's quite nice.'

'A friend of yours, is he? Does he live round here?'

'Not very close,' he said, evading the first question.

'Well, why not ask him to tea? I'm sure Mummy wouldn't mind, if you'd like to.'

'I could,' said Philip.

Although his name was often coupled with Thomas's in the jeers of the gang, the two boys had not spoken to each other since the day Philip didn't climb the roof. It had somehow seemed necessary to prove to Gordon that they were not friends, not in the least; and now he wondered why. He thought he had had enough of doing things because of Gordon. He thought he would ask Thomas.

They went inside. Martha was just going to bed, and started a fresh burst of tears because there was no teddy to put her head on. She usually slept curled sideways, using it as a pillow. Philip offered his, but Martha said it didn't feel nice. Eventually her mother persuaded her to accept an old fur glove.

'Couldn't we put a notice in the paper shop?' suggested Philip. 'Offering a reward, perhaps, if anyone returns it?'

His father thought this a good idea. 'It might cheer Martha up. And it would be worth a bit to get it back.'

'I think it's rather unlikely that anyone will find it now,' said his mother.

'Well,' said Philip, 'if someone had taken it for fun, they might just drop it again quite soon.'

For instance (this time he admitted it to himself) someone like Gordon and the gang.

Eight

It was four o'clock. They were all coming out of school. Philip put on a spurt that took him to Thomas Fearn's side; it was easier to speak while walking along than to go up to him deliberately in the playground.

'Whereabouts do you live?' he asked.

Thomas looked surprised, and named a road.

'Is that far?'

'Not very.'

'I live just up Hilton Avenue.'

'Yes?' said Thomas without much apparent interest.

'You could come round one day,' said Philip. 'If you liked.'

'I could?'

'Yes, if you wanted to.'

After a pause Thomas asked: 'What about your mother?'

'Oh, it would be all right, she said so, if it was tomorrow or Friday.'

('Can I have a boy to tea?' he had said.

'What boy?'

'His name's Thomas.'

His mother had been doubtful. 'That's all very well, but you can't ask just one, can you? It'll mean the whole lot.'

'Which lot?'

'Gordon Downie and the rest.'

'Oh no, they don't like him. They won't want to come. He doesn't belong to any lot actually.')

'Hum,' said Thomas Fearn.

Philip looked at him tentatively. They had almost reached Hilton Avenue, where they would have to turn different ways.

'Tomorrow then?' said Thomas.

'Yes. All right. Tomorrow,' said Philip with satisfaction.

When it was time to go home next day he didn't hurry. It would be better to let Gordon and friends get well away; then he and Thomas could walk along in their own time and in peace. He was last to leave the cloakroom, and looked for Thomas on the path outside, but he wasn't there. He wasn't waiting under the arch or by the railings. Philip wandered round growing increasingly puzzled, and finally returned to his classroom.

'Do you want something?' asked Mr Grant, who was pinning a poster to the wall.

'Only Thomas Fearn, sir.'

'He's long since gone. So should you be.'

'Yes, sir.'

Thomas must have decided not to come after all. Philip started his solitary walk home in a black mood. The sound of his heels on the pavement turned into a wordless grumble, plaintive and meandering. He put his feet down harder and harder to give it force, only stopping when he thought he was getting a headache.

As he passed the newsagents' he looked sourly at the card in the window. LOST, Teddy Bear. It had been there four days and nobody had come to claim the twenty pence reward, though he had seen James and Neil nudge each other craftily as they read about it. Presumably twenty pence was not enough to tempt the gang, or more likely the teddy was in some inaccessible spot such as the bottom of the canal. And suddenly he remembered how he had seen them kicking something along the towpath the day the toy had vanished. He froze with rage, recalling their laughter. He was sure his guess was right.

Then he thought it might not be as inaccessible as all that. The canal was quite shallow in some places; if the teddy was visible it would perhaps be possible to fish it out. He could go and see.

A new energy quickened his pace. When he reached his own close he went past; he was not in the mood for unnecessary delays. His mother would want Thomas's absence explained, and she might insist on his staying at home in case Thomas turned up later. He held his breath until he was safely round the corner at the end of Hilton Avenue.

On the first stretch of towpath he was again in danger of being seen, either from the back windows of the flat or from the garden. He didn't think his mother was as fond of looking out as he was; all the same he ran. He had watched the gang kick the teddy (or tin can) until they were out of sight of the back windows, so he needn't begin his search until he in his turn was out of sight. As soon as a bunch of small trees intervened between him and the flats he slowed down.

The canal was extremely murky. Even picking his way along the edge of the bank and looking as hard as he could, he made out very little of the bottom. A submerged petrol drum caught his eye because of its label, but that was all. He could only hope the bear's honey-coloured fur would help to make it visible.

He began to wonder how far to go. He couldn't continue indefinitely with a search based on a guess. He saw the lock ahead; he thought he would turn back there. He followed the curve of the bank round to the paved edge of the lock, and looked inside. A gas stove had been added to the rubbish since his last visit. There was also a large ball of sodden greyish waste, to which his eye returned in fascinated disgust. It reminded him of what the plumber had once extracted from a blocked pipe at home; that had had a sort of tail, which made it look like a dead rat, and this seemed to have limbs . . . did have limbs – it was Martha's teddy!

His heart pounded with triumph. He had been right, he had been right; everything had happened as he had supposed. Now all he had to do was get it out.

He lost half his enthusiasm when he looked at the rusty ladder fixed to the far side of the lock; and he lost the rest when he realised that to reach the ladder he would have to walk across the top of the closed lock gates. Pure defiance drove him after that. He would get the teddy, filthy and unrecognisable as it was; it shouldn't just be left here to rot.

He chose the higher pair of gates, which meant there was a drop only on one side, to the rubbish; on the other the water came nearly to the top. They seemed firm enough when he tried them with his hand. The towpath was deserted behind, and in front the only figure, though approaching, was too far away to matter. He pulled his lower lip between his teeth and took his first step.

When he reached the other side his lip was sore. He attacked the ladder straight away, finding as he descended into the depths of the lock that he could only keep out thoughts of metal weakened by rust if he allowed into his head two untimely lines of poetry. *And a thousand thousand slimy things Lived on; and so did I. And a thousand thousand slimy things* . . . He was terribly afraid that when he lifted the teddy there would be wriggling movement underneath.

The toy was a yard from the bottom of the ladder. Just beside him the stream of water pouring through the hole in the doors lost itself amid the rubbish. He trod on a mattress that squelched. Then the teddy's ear was in his hand and he pulled. There were no wriggling things. Realising he would need both hands for the ladder, he threw the teddy as hard as he could; it landed up above, and he followed it up himself.

It had a drowned seaweedy smell. He sat down some distance from it in the scrubby grass, his legs flopping straight as he looked across the canal. The trudging figure on the towpath was much nearer now. It was Thomas Fearn.

'Hallo!' yelled Philip.

Thomas glanced at him with no surprise and came to his own side of the lock. 'What were you doing?' he asked.

'Oh, did you see me?'

'I saw you cross. I wondered what for.'

'I had to get this out.'

'That?' said Thomas, peering incredulously.

'It's my sister's.' He saw a good deal more explanation would be needed to justify his act to Thomas. 'What are you doing along here anyway?' he asked.

'I thought you were expecting me.'

'I'd given you up. And I was never expecting you along here.' Philip felt rather muddled. 'This is a terribly long way round from school.' He could scarcely guess what complication of streets Thomas must have passed through in order to be coming along the towpath in this direction.

'It's a short way round from my home.'

'I didn't know you were going home first.'

'Oh well. It meant a quieter walk. No point being set on if you can avoid it.'

Thomas, Philip realised with surprise, was even more cautious than himself. He didn't mind admitting it either; but that was all of a piece with the rest of his character.

'We can go together now,' said Philip, 'only I'll have to get back to your side first.' He looked at the lock gates.

'I wouldn't if I were you,' said Thomas.

'What would you do?'

'Go back a bit and get on to the road.'

'But then I'd have to stay on the road.'

'Yes.'

'So we can't go together.'

'We'll be going the same way,' said Thomas, unmoved.

'Will you wait for me at the end of the towpath?'

Thomas nodded. Philip picked up the teddy and found that the road came near to the canal a little further back. He climbed the fence and turned towards his home, singing the chorus of Loch Lomond.

He was relieved to find that Thomas did wait. As they turned the corner into Hilton Avenue Philip told him the story of the teddy bear.

'It could do with a wash,' said Thomas.

'Yes, I know,' said Philip anxiously. It had just occurred to him that if his mother saw and smelt the teddy in its present state she might throw it away without further ado. 'It is washable.'

'Yes?'

'I think I might wash it a bit myself. I expect I can sneak it inside.'

For the time being he concealed it in the communal cupboard under the stairs at the bottom of the close.

'Where on earth have you been?' asked his mother when she let them in.

'Oh sorry,' said Philip. 'We came a long way round.'

She welcomed Thomas in a friendlier manner and said she was just getting tea. (It was visitors' tea, in his honour, an hour earlier than usual.) Martha was nowhere to be seen. Philip showed Thomas some of his toys and left him looking at his stamp collection while he slipped out again for the teddy and took it into the bathroom. After being immersed in a basin of suds its original colour returned, and he was trying to squeeze it out a little when his mother came and rattled the door.

'Hurry up, Philip! What are you running all that water for? Tea's ready, and you should be looking after your guest.'

He drew back the bolt. 'I found Martha's teddy,' he began, but his mother had already seen it lolling against the taps and dripping loudly on the floor. After that she was so busy rinsing it and cramming it into the spin drier that he managed to evade an exact description of the place where it had been found. 'Along by the towpath,' he truthfully said as he joined Thomas at the tea table.

While they were eating his mother made one or two attempts at conversation with Thomas, but the answers she received seemed to discourage her. He had even less to say for himself than John Eccles, and she had never particularly taken to John.

Martha came in. Philip told her to go into the kitchen and look up. She obeyed, puzzled; and the sight of her bear spreadeagled on the drying rack made her gasp.

'Is it my teddy?' she said in a small voice.

'Yes,' said Philip, and she started a wild clamour for it to be got down immediately. Thomas listened in astonishment and withdrew even further into himself.

'I don't know if you have any younger brothers or sisters?' said Mrs Gray with a harassed smile. ('Martha, I tell you it's *wet*. Sit down and have some tea, look, you can have sausages, you like sausages. Philip, *need* you have drawn her attention to it just now?')

'Yes, have you?' Philip asked with interest. Thomas shook his head.

'Well, she's not always as bad as this,' said Philip, thinking that was what his mother wanted Thomas to realise. But Martha, affronted, increased the volume of her complaints and his mother didn't look at all pleased. Thomas addressed himself severely to his food and Philip did the same, thinking the sooner they were finished the sooner they could go out.

'What time have you got to be home, Thomas?' asked Mrs Gray as they went.

'By dark.'

'Oh – well, I'd like Philip back here a bit before that. Say in an hour's time, Philip. Where will you be?'

'Along by the canal, towards the river.'

He had quite a job getting Thomas past the painted GORDON DOWNIE OK on the wall. Thomas stopped dead when he saw it and said: 'Do we have to go this way?'

'Why not? They don't own the towpath.'

'I dare say they think they do.'

'I often come here when they're not around. I've got a secret place further along.'

'How secret?' asked Thomas sceptically.

'Well – I thought I could show you.'

Thomas shrugged. 'All right. If we're caught we're caught I suppose.'

They saw nothing of the gang. Thomas picked his way down the tangled slope behind Philip, and swung round the fence-post with great precision.

'You see,' said Philip.

Thomas looked at the mill. Then he said: 'What's to stop Gordon's lot coming here too?'

'They don't know there's any way in. There wasn't one, until I made it. I took a lot of barbed wire off this post.'

'Hmm,' said Thomas. He eyed the flight of steps. 'Can we go inside?'

'Yes, of course.' Philip led the way. When they were in he closed the door behind Thomas and waited for him to speak.

'No wonder they fenced it off,' said Thomas. 'It's dropping to bits.'

'Only the roof. The hole in the floor's meant to be there; you can see it must have had a trap-door once.'

Thomas grunted, but went on examining everything in a very interested way. He bounced once or twice on the floor-boards and had a look out of the window.

'Good view across the river,' he said. 'What if you want to find out what's happening nearer home?'

Something about his double-edged comment pleased Philip; after a moment he realised it was the word home.

'There's a hole in the door,' he said, noticing one beside the broken lock.

'Yes,' said Thomas, trying it. 'You can see a bit through that.'

He prowled back to the window and they both gazed out for a few moments in silence.

'It's funny,' said Philip, 'this mill hasn't been used for years, and yet the water will have to keep running over the weir for ever and ever.'

'I doubt the water cares,' said Thomas.

Something bumped in Philip's pocket and he remembered that he had had other plans besides showing Thomas the mill. 'There's an old railway tunnel a bit further along,' he said. 'It's quite easy to get to. I thought we might explore inside. I brought a torch.'

'All right,' said Thomas, looking through the spyhole before he opened the door.

Half-way to the tunnel they had to jump a stream that came splashing down the leafy bank and ran across the strip of pebbles. The sight of it made them thirsty; they drank from cupped hands. The water was clear and icy cold.

'Where does this tunnel go?' said Thomas when they reached it.

'The other end's over beyond the towpath. I've been in there with Gordon and the rest, but you can't get right through; it's blocked.' He switched on his torch.

They reached the block quite quickly. It was a man-made barrier and it wasn't complete. There was a hole at one side large enough for them to get through. Philip approached it cautiously with the torch; not that he expected the gang to be lurking on the other side, but there was something a bit unnerving about the narrow black gap.

'Oh!' he said.

'What?' said Thomas. 'Let me see.'

'It's nothing really, only it's blocked again.'

There was a second barrier a few yards beyond the first. They were obviously the work of the same person, both put together from a hotchpotch of railway sleepers, wooden crates, tea-chests, even an old square-sided cistern. The boys stepped through the opening and stood between them.

'Why two, I wonder?' said Thomas.

The second barrier had no gaps at all.

'It's like a little room,' said Philip. 'It is a little room! That's the doorway.'

'And that's the door.' Thomas pointed to a couple of tea-chests lying beside the wall of the tunnel. 'Put one on top of the other and they'd just fit.'

'And then . . . hey, then it would simply look like one barrier. Nobody'd know it was hollow. It's a sort of priest's hole!'

'Crook's hole, more likely. You could hide stolen goods in here.'

'Oh – do you think – ?'

'I don't suppose anyone uses it now. But I bet you that's what it was built for.'

Whatever it had been built for it had the feel of an old, forgotten place. There was a crumpled sheet of newspaper in one corner, with a date four years old. Thomas tried putting the tea-chests in the gap, and the top one wouldn't go; the barrier must have shifted slightly as it aged, and the tea-chest was an inch too high.

'Give me a hand,' panted Thomas, 'and I'll try it end on.'

Philip hung back. The bottom tea-chest fitted too snugly; he didn't like to see Thomas filling the only remaining space, it reminded him of a story he had once read called *The Cask of Amontillado*; what if they walled themselves up and couldn't get out? 'Are you sure . . .' he began.

'There,' said Thomas. 'Just the job.' He grinned in the torchlight. 'Cosy, isn't it?'

Philip's answering smile was brief, produced mostly in response to the fact that it was the first time he had seen Thomas's face look anything but solemn. 'Let's go back now,' he said.

The tea-chests were easily moved after all. Looking along the way they had come Philip found he could see reflected daylight, a pale glimmer on the curving wall of the tunnel.

Thomas wouldn't let him leave at once. 'We haven't shut the door,' he said. 'This is one secret that needn't be left for everyone to find.' And while Philip held the torch he put the tea-chests in position again, so that the barrier was complete.

As they went back by the river's edge Philip tried to forget Thomas's latter remark. He knew what it meant; the mill was a good place, but the gang were bound to discover it. The thought made him fierce. He felt like writing KEEP OUT, with a skull and crossbones, on the door of the upper room. He knew there would really be no point, but he still wanted to do something to show them – the gang, and Thomas too.

He saw from his watch that there was no time to linger at the mill. On their way home Thomas noticed the swinging rope.

'They made me go on that,' said Philip; and suddenly he knew what he wanted to do. 'I'm going to cut it down.'

'You're what?' said Thomas.

'I'm going to cut it down.' He was scrambling up the bank, climbing the tree. He drew the rope up into his hand and opened his penknife.

'You're crazy,' said Thomas. He began to walk on.

'Wait!' called Philip, sawing madly. 'Wait!'

His knife wasn't sharp enough. He was making no impression on the rope. And Thomas wasn't waiting. One of the gang might come along at any moment, and a fat lot of good Thomas would be, thought Philip bitterly.

It was no good; he couldn't even cut through one strand. He dropped the rope, climbed down himself and ran after Thomas.

'I couldn't do it,' he panted.

'I'm not surprised,' said Thomas severely. 'For goodness' sake.'

When they reached Philip's home they said goodbye at the entrance to the close. Thomas didn't want to come in, and Philip didn't press him. He was still feeling flattened by his failure with the rope.

He found his parents and Martha all talking hard.

'*Why* can't I go to the wedding?' Martha was saying.

'Because you haven't been invited,' replied her mother in tones of patience wearing thin.

'I've never been to a wedding. It's not fair.'

'Nobody is going to the wedding, so it's perfectly fair.'

Philip saw that his father was holding an opened envelope that must have come by the second post.

'Who's getting married?' he asked.

'Amanda Glover. You remember the Glovers.'

'Oh yes.' They lived in Grantham.

'It's very kind of them,' Mr Gray said to his wife, 'but I suppose you're right.'

'Of course I'm right,' she snapped. 'Come along, Martha. It's time for your bath.'

The room was a lot quieter after she had taken Martha out.

'What's very kind of the Glovers? Have they invited you and Mummy to the wedding?' asked Philip.

'Yes, but not just that; they've offered to put us up for a couple of nights, before and after, because of the distance we'd be travelling.' He sighed.

'Won't you go?'

'I shouldn't think so. Too difficult all round. It's a pity, it would have given Mummy a little break.'

Philip agreed that his mother seemed to need a break, though he wasn't sure exactly what from.

'Has your friend gone home?' asked his father.

'Yes.'

'I'd have liked to meet him. Well, another day perhaps. Did you have a good time?'

'Yes. Yes, we did.'

Nine

Martha was extremely upset about being excluded from the wedding invitation, and next morning she told Alison and Joan all about it. Later in the day Mrs Downie mentioned it to Mrs Gray, who said of course they wouldn't be going, because of the children. Mrs Downie thereupon astonished her by saying that she would have them; and was so earnest about the pleasure it would give her and the lack of trouble it would be that Mrs Gray found herself accepting, with gratitude.

Martha took the news quite well; she liked the idea of sleeping with Alison. Philip, on the other hand, couldn't conceal his dismay.

'Couldn't we stay with someone else?' he asked his father.

'Well, not really; not now we've said yes to Mrs Downie. In any case, there isn't anyone else, is there?'

'Mrs Macleod . . . Thomas Fearn . . .' But Philip didn't take these suggestions seriously, and he could see his father didn't either.

'I thought you got on fairly well with Gordon?'

'Not now.'

'Oh. Well, that's a pity. You couldn't make the effort to smooth things over, just for two nights? He seems a decent enough person; I should think he'd meet you half-way. The pair of you ought to be able to have fun.'

Philip said nothing.

'It's going to rather spoil it for Mummy if you continue to view the prospect with *quite* so much alarm and despondency.'

Philip managed a small smile.

'It won't be that bad, will it, old chap?' His father had the beginnings of such a look of relief that Philip was somehow able to hold on to his smile.

'No, I suppose not,' he said.

'Good for you,' said his father, and ruffled his hair.

Philip went away to the mill soon afterwards, where he sat thinking gloomy thoughts. He could no more see himself smoothing things over with Gordon than he could see Gordon meeting him half-way. In any case, surely it was for him to meet Gordon half-way – only if one person met another, presumably the other person met the one, just as much? Still, which ever way you put it it was equally unlikely.

He looked out of the window and got a shock. On the far side of the river, where the ground flattened at the bottom of the green slope, were James and Neil. He ducked out of sight at once and cautiously edged back for another look. They were throwing stones at a floating petrol drum. There was no sign of the rest of the gang.

He wondered how long they had been there. The drum was stuck on top of the weir, and they kept on throwing until they had dislodged it and sent it over. Then they followed it downstream a little way, turning back while they were still in Philip's range of vision. Then they climbed up the slope to the canal bridge, and after that he couldn't have seen them any more without sticking his head out of the window, which he certainly wasn't going to do.

A little time passed. They might be home by now. They might equally well be lingering on the piece of towpath that Philip had to cover in order to get home himself.

He wished Thomas were with him; his dour comments would be heartening. He remembered his own brave words about the gang not owning the towpath. The fact was that he had never met any of the gang while trespassing alone on their territory, and he didn't much want to begin with James and Neil.

'Then you'd better go a different way,' he said to himself in Thomas's voice.

Almost immediately he thought of two possibilities. He could follow the route he had discovered with his parents, away from the river and home via the streets of houses his mother had liked. The trouble with that was that for a short distance on the track he would be visible from the point on the towpath where the track branched off, and since this was near the swinging rope it was a likely place for James and Neil to be. The other way he could go was upstream along the edge of the river. Although he hadn't yet been further than the mouth of the tunnel he knew the strip of pebbles didn't end there; it was worth a try. He would only be visible if they were standing on the bridge leaning over the parapet, and he could check the parapet before he started. This he did, putting his head out of the window. There were no heads looking over.

The strip of pebbles went all the way to the canal bridge. He got through the bridge along a ledge of masonry which ran beside the water and just above it. At the other side he was able to scramble on to the bank, which was rough grass here instead of jungle. He felt safe along this stretch, overlooked only by the blind side of the canal. He was coming up to the road bridge where he and his father had met the woman who fed the cats. The road wasn't nearly so high above the river as the canal, and he was able to scramble up the stone-work of the bridge and over the parapet. From there it was an easy walk home. He saw nothing of James and Neil, so probably his precautions had been unnecessary.

The next day he sought Thomas out in the playground. He still had to do this if he wanted to speak to him; Thomas never took the initiative.

'My parents are going away on Thursday. I've got to spend two nights at Gordon's,' he said.

'More fool you.'

He realized Thomas had taken the news to indicate that he was back in favour with the gang.

'It's not my fault,' he said. 'I didn't want to. Mrs Downie offered. I don't suppose Gordon's very pleased either, come to that.'

'Humph,' said Thomas.

Philip wished very hard that Thomas would return his invitation to tea and ask him home on Thursday or Friday. But all Thomas gave him was some advice.

'Keep your hands behind your back. No provocation.'

'Are you a pacifist?' asked Philip curiously.

'Only when I've no weapons,' said Thomas.

Philip went to school as usual on Thursday. Resigned, he asked if he should take his pyjamas.

'There's no need, love. I'll give all your things to Mrs Downie with Martha's.'

'Don't forget her teddy.'

'Of course not. It was clever of you to find that for her; I don't know what she'd have done without it this week-end.'

His mother seemed better for the break already, he thought.

'Do you want any toys or books yourself?' she asked.

'No thanks.' Nothing he valued was going within range of Gordon. And he would keep a particular eye on the teddy, though he didn't somehow think the gang would touch that again.

At four o'clock Philip lingered as long as he could in the cloakroom, and was finally rewarded with a peaceful walk home. It felt very strange to pass his own close. The windows of their flat were shut, but what could be glimpsed of the inside looked just the same as usual.

He arrived at the Downies' on the tail of a row. Gordon was standing red-faced, with Alison and Martha an interested audience, while his mother said: 'Tomorrow you see you remember your manners, and don't go rushing off! Oh, here he is. Come in, Philip. I'm just making some tea, and would you like a spam roll?'

The first evening passed better than Philip had expected. Mrs Downie was a very hospitable person. Mr Downie was large and silent; he said hallo to Philip and then settled to watch television, rousing himself only once to hit Gordon when he and Alison were fighting over a chair.

In the morning Mrs Downie cooked a large breakfast, and urged Philip to eat more than he easily could. Alison and Martha ran about in pyjamas and the radio played loudly. They were late leaving; Mrs Downie thrust bars of chocolate into their pockets ('there's your play pieces') and told them they'd better run.

'I'm not waiting,' said Gordon as soon as they were outside. Philip could run quite fast, but he let Gordon draw ahead. No provocation, he thought to himself.

At four o'clock Gordon came up to him in the cloakroom. 'None of your hanging about now,' he said. 'We've to get home together.'

Philip wished gloomily that Mrs Downie didn't care so much for good manners. Today there was no escaping the gang, and they gave him a rough journey. He was hustled, poked, prodded and kicked. If Gordon had been his only tormentor he might have hit back, but as it was he couldn't help seeing the sense of Thomas's advice. He longed for a friendly adult; if only Gordon's father would come along, or Mr Grant, instead of mothers so busy watching their toddlers they had no attention to spare for a bunch of scuffling boys.

Then he did recognize a figure approaching from behind with a shopping bag. It was Mrs Macleod. Surely she would notice what was going on? She knew him, and Gordon, probably some of the others as well; she wouldn't just pass by without a glance.

She was getting nearer and nearer. She was on the other side of the road and the gang hadn't noticed. Philip felt suddenly bold; he wouldn't let her think him completely helpless. James aimed another kick at his bruised shins. 'Leave me alone!' he cried shrilly; and he stamped on James's toes and gave Neil a violent push.

Next moment they were all on top of him, and soon he no longer had the choice of fighting back because all his limbs were held. No voice intervened to stop them. In the end it was Gordon himself who said, 'All right, that's enough. He's learned his lesson.' When he scrambled to his feet and looked round for Mrs Macleod she was tiny in the distance, hurrying on towards her home.

They were quite kind after that; they allowed him to brush his clothes down and hold a handkerchief to his cut lip. They began dispersing to their various homes before they reached Gordon's close. As Philip and Gordon climbed the steps Mrs Downie opened the door.

'Come on in, the pair of you,' she said; and when they had done so: 'Look at you! Just look at you!'

'Philip fell,' said Gordon quickly.

He received a resounding slap. 'Now don't start!' said his mother. 'I know perfectly well what you've been doing; Mrs

85

Macleod told me. She saw the whole bunch of you down the road, fighting!'

It was quite clear that her anger included them both. Philip opened his mouth, but couldn't think of anything to say. Gordon looked sullen.

'Rolling about on the pavement!' continued Mrs Downie. 'If you wanted to fight you should have waited until you were out of your school clothes. Philip, you'd better let me have your jersey and trousers to wash at once. And your lip needs a plaster.'

Philip wished he had stuck to Thomas's advice. Though even if he had not provoked the gang, Mrs Macleod might still have hurried by without noticing what was really happening.

After he had changed he stood by the bedroom window fingering the plaster on his lip and looking out. It was strange to see the familiar view and yet not be at home.

Gordon came in. 'Does it hurt?' he asked.

'A bit,' said Philip, surprised into truth.

'You'll have to remember not to smile,' said Gordon. 'That should be easy enough.'

Philip couldn't help returning his teasing grin, and then clapping a hand to the plaster.

'What did I tell you?' Gordon grinned wider. 'Come on. There's some tea made.'

Philip's parents telephoned that evening.

'Well,' said his father, 'how are you?'

'All right.'

'Everything going smoothly?'

'Yes.'

'We should be back in time for tea tomorrow.'

'Oh. Good.'

'I thought we might go and look at a house on Sunday. There's one for sale in Rowan Drive. Number six.'

'Oh.'

'Philip, are you sure you're all right?'

'Yes.'

'You sound rather odd.'

'I'm fine.'

'Well, I hope you are. Here's Mummy now.'

'Philip,' said his mother, 'is anything wrong?'

'No. Of course not.' He felt hot and awkward.

'Are you quite sure?'

'Yes. Yes. I'm fine.' Gordon caught his eye and winked.

He was glad to hand the telephone over to Martha, whose conversation ran: 'Me and Alison are sleeping on a bed that folds up. – What? – What, Mummy? – What? – Oh. – No I haven't finished yet, I want to tell Mummy a thing . . . ummm . . . Alison and me have got a bed that folds up. – What?'

Then Mrs Downie had a turn. 'I hear you're going house-hunting,' she said to Philip afterwards. 'Rowan Drive. Very posh.'

'Where is it?'

'Up the hill, on beyond the new flats.'

It would be one of the houses his mother had liked the look of, he supposed. He might take an interest later; the main thing at the moment was that his parents would be home tomorrow in time for tea. Only a morning and an afternoon left to go. And he was beginning to think Gordon had meant it when he said, 'He's had enough.'

Ten

The weather was fine next morning. Gordon pushed back his chair as soon as he had finished breakfast and announced that he was going out.

'Wait for Philip,' said his mother.

'No, it's all right, I don't –' Philip began.

'I'm only rounding up the gang. I'll be back,' said Gordon.

Philip thought this was an excuse, made to enable Gordon to get away. He must allow his contentment to show if so; he didn't want Gordon to be in trouble for neglecting him again. He ate his large breakfast with enjoyment, planning a visit to the shops with the little girls.

He had only been in the back garden a few minutes and hadn't yet asked them what they thought of the idea, when Gordon appeared at the top of the steps.

'Coming, Philip?'

He hesitated.

'*Come* on!' yelled Gordon.

Mrs Downie opened a window and leaned out to shake a duster. 'Mind you're back for your meal, you two!' she called.

Philip shrugged off his doubts and ran up the steps. The others were all waiting out in the road. He didn't much like the look of delight on Neil's face, but Robert said hallo in his ordinary gruff voice and Alastair nodded to him.

They set off down the road. They all seemed to know where they were going, and Philip didn't like to ask. They crossed the road near the canal bridge, but instead of turning off along the towpath James, who was in the lead, walked firmly on. When Philip followed he found himself tripping over Neil's feet. He fell against someone else, was pushed back, and found himself being bounced from one to the other while Neil said, 'He doesn't seem to want to come this way!' and James replied, 'I wonder why that could be?'

Then Gordon caught him and set him roughly on his feet. 'Mind out now,' he told the others. 'We can't give him back to his parents *covered* in plaster.'

They all laughed. Philip just managed to stop himself touching his lip. He wished he had thought of taking the horrible plaster off that morning.

They were, of course, going along the towpath after all.

'Are we stopping by the rope?' James asked Gordon.

'Yes, we might as well.'

'Philip hasn't been on it for ages,' said Neil unctuously.

Philip wondered whether it would be any good refusing his turn. They reached the rope and he looked at it, angry with himself for not cutting it down when he had had the chance. Then he stiffened and looked again. The rope was different at the top; it was whiskery. He had thought he couldn't cut through one strand, but he must have managed it after all; or else it had worn through since. One strand was certainly severed now. It was unravelling in both directions, and the remaining strands had come untwisted.

'Who's first?' said Gordon.

'I think Philip should be first,' said Neil.

Philip swallowed, and his voice came out much louder than he intended. 'I'm not going on it. It's not safe.'

'He's scared!' jeered James.

'Well, we knew that,' said Gordon impatiently. 'Let someone else go.'

'It's not safe,' Philip repeated. His face was burning. He didn't know how he could point out the frayed part of the rope without the guilt in his voice giving him away. It looked so obvious to him; surely someone else must notice it too?

'Look, shut up,' advised Robert. 'You don't have to go on it. Just shut up.'

'*I'll* show baby how safe it is,' exclaimed Neil, scrambling up the bank. 'James, give me a push.'

Ten seconds later he was moving off with a showy display of speed, and two minutes after that he was in the canal.

Philip watched in a kind of suspended horror as they pulled him out. It happened not to be one of the deeper parts of the canal – no thanks to him, thought Philip, supposing he would have been a murderer if Neil had drowned – most of the rope had sunk, but there was still the bit tied to the branch, and presumably if one knew how to look one could tell it had been cut –

'Don't get your hands dirty, will you!' said James; and the group round the sodden, streaming Neil all turned and glared at Philip. If his face had been red before it was nothing to what it was now. Neil, who was mopping his eyes with James's handkerchief, stopped.

'You knew that was going to happen,' he said hoarsely.

Philip ran. He ran in the only direction open to him; further along the towpath. He had the advantage of surprise, and he used his full speed, but he knew he couldn't outrun the whole gang for very long. Without making a conscious choice he found himself taking the riverside track, and as they came roaring after him he left the track and slithered down through the undergrowth to the mill. Round the fence-post with practised smoothness, up the steps and into his room, the door shut behind him, he crouched at the spyhole with his heart thudding and waves of chequered blackness obscuring his vision.

They seemed to go on crashing about in the undergrowth for hours. Every time they came near the fence he shivered; once he heard them discussing whether he could have climbed over, but nobody thought to look for a way round the end. Eventually they said something about dry clothes for Neil, and he gathered they were all going to escort him home and help pacify his mother. The voices withdrew into the distance and Philip sat down weakly on the floor.

He wondered what they would tell Neil's mother. Not the truth, he was sure – if indeed they had guessed it correctly. They might think the whole catastrophe had been intentional; Neil might even think Philip had purposely provoked him into using the rope first. It was just the kind of thing Neil himself would do. Would they believe him if he denied it? In any case they would still be angry because he hadn't told them about the fraying, and because he had weakened the rope with his knife in the first place. If they caught him they would probably throw him into the canal.

The sun shone through the roof on to his outstretched legs. Now that it had withstood their search the mill felt very safe. He looked round the solid walls with affection. He would wait a bit longer to make sure they were really gone and then dash for the Downies' house. The sacks prickled the backs of his knees, but it would have been too much trouble to shift his position.

He woke in a panic. How could he have slept, how could he? His watch showed that he had been unconscious for over an hour. Anyone could have sneaked up on him in that time; anything could have happened.

Yet apparently nothing had. He checked window and spyhole and saw nothing alarming. His heart gradually began to slow down. His mouth was very dry, and he thought he would go along to the stream where he and Thomas had drunk. He opened the door and went down the steps, his limbs still clumsy with sleep.

He was drinking when he heard the shout.

'There he is!'

He straightened and stared wildly round him.

'Down there!'

They were looking over the parapet of the canal bridge, their heads outlined darkly against the sky; James and Alastair, and the rest were joining them.

He was terribly visible. He couldn't return to the mill or hide in the tunnel because they would see. Now that they knew there had to be a way past the fence it was only a matter of time until they found it. He must run, but where? Not up to the track, because they would be waiting for him. Then with a rush of relief he remembered the route he had discovered a few days earlier when he was evading James and Neil.

They thought it was odd when he started upstream towards the bridge.

'Where's he going?'

'Hey, Philip! What's the idea?'

'Spit on him!'

No spit landed. He stepped on to the ledge of stonework and then he was under the bridge, and they could no longer see him. And wouldn't be able to when he emerged, either, because as he had noticed before it was the blind side of the canal that overlooked the next stretch of river. He would climb up onto the road bridge when he reached it, but he didn't know if he dared follow the road home. Although they couldn't see him they might guess what he was doing, and run along the towpath in time to intercept him at the crossroads. He might turn the other way, towards the Ladyhill Road – that would fox them.

He jogged along the river bank, not quite running because he was afraid he might trip on the tussocks of grass. When he heard the triumphant shouts he couldn't at first believe them. Then he groaned aloud. He had been so sure they would stay on the towpath; he had forgotten that they could come down the slope below the tower flats. There they all were on the opposite bank of the river, making for the same road as him; and they had smooth grass to run on, and an open gateway in the wall ahead.

He stopped dead. He was so nearly at the bridge that he could see through its arch to the fence of the new gasworks. The gang were nearly at the road too; if he turned back now they would run him down on this uneven ground.

'We've got him!' cried James exultantly.

He jerked into movement and ran towards the road bridge. He had noticed something else about the view through the arch. On the other side, between the gasworks fence and the river, was another strip of pebbles like the one by the mill. It looked all right for running; firm and smooth.

He got through the bridge along another narrow ledge. He had confused them again, and they lost some time trying to climb down on the other side of the road; it was only possible on the side where he had climbed up before. Then they had to come one at a time through the bridge, which delayed them further. The strip of pebbles fulfilled its promise, and he ran and ran.

In the end it was another bridge that stopped him. He guessed from the look of it that this one carried the railway. There was no way through; he had to climb the embankment. He paused for a panting, wavering moment at the top (he was right about the railway) and saw his pursuers strung out behind him with yards between each. James was in the lead, with Gordon next. Neil didn't seem to be there at all. He dashed across the lines and paused again to get his bearings. The railway ran straight and endless, master of the irregular ground; he could see to the refuse incineration plant in one direction, and to the Ladyhill road in the other. In front of him lay a cindery waste of barren hills and rubbish-filled hollows that stretched as far as the derelict factory buildings fringing the tar distillery. He had a pain in his chest and he knew he couldn't run much further. The buildings were his only hope.

As he started down the embankment he heard a wonderful noise. A train was coming. He had gone a few yards from the bottom when it rumbled by, and he spared a moment to turn his head. He could see nobody; they must be fuming on the other side of the line. It was a long goods train. He blessed it as he went dodging on.

He came round a hump and found he had to cross an old railway siding. Then suddenly the abandoned buildings were all round him. He forced himself to pass the first two open doorways, and entered the third. It was an empty shed; he did the best he could, and got behind the door.

The blood in his ears was louder than the voices when they arrived a moment later. Waiting for the train to pass had obviously bunched the gang together again.

'Now,' said Gordon, 'we'll do it properly. He's somewhere in here for certain, and we've got to get him this time. James, you're fastest – you go and check that he didn't get through to the road, and then stay by the gate in case he tries to run that way. Robert, you can search that way; Alastair, you go that way, and Malcolm that way, and I'll stay here where I can watch you all.'

They scattered. Philip thought that at least they couldn't throw him into the canal here. And he'd been right about Neil; his mother must have kept him at home. There was still James though.

The search was almost on him. Why was it that once you had started running the idea of being caught was so utterly dreadful? He had noticed the same before in chases begun for fun –

'I thought I'd told you boys not to come in here!' said an angry voice.

After a moment Gordon replied. 'We were chasing someone, you see, and he led us this way. All right, Philip,' he shouted, 'game ended. You'll have to come out.'

Philip stayed rigid. He heard the other searchers gathering.

'Is this all of you then?' said the man.

'No, he's still hiding – the one we were after, I mean. Philip!'

'You sure he exists?' said the man roughly.

'Of course he does. I'll just look – '

'You will not,' said the man. 'Go on, the lot of you. I've had enough. If I see you in here again I'll speak to your parents, and I mean that.'

The footsteps receded. Minutes passed. Philip was just beginning to think it would be safe to move when he heard heavy feet returning.

'Right,' called the man's voice, 'are you going to come out now and save me the trouble of looking for you?'

Philip emerged, walking automatically. He felt numb.

'So you *were* there!' said the man.

'Yes.'

The man motioned him in the direction of the gate. As they went towards it he suddenly looked more closely at Philip.

'You were in here that other day. You're the one from England, aren't you?'

'Yes.'

'Aye. I thought so. Well, your pals have gone. One of them asked me the time and they all bolted. After their dinners, I expect. You'll be wanting yours too.'

They had reached the gate. Philip looked up towards the refuse incineration plant. The road was empty as far as the brow of the hill. 'Yes,' he said, starting off in that direction because the man expected him to.

It was gone one o'clock. If the gang were really all in their homes, eating, it was the obvious moment for him to go too. So obvious that Gordon must have thought of it. He would never just sit down to his food and leave Philip free to walk in at the door; not after the relentless chase of the morning. Someone would be left guarding the crossroads, or if they weren't prepared to go without their own meal (the rumbling emptiness in Philip's stomach made him doubt that anyone would be) Gordon only had to keep looking out of the Downies' living-room window, and he would see Philip as soon as he topped the hill. As Philip considered all this his legs went slower and slower.

Really the best way to approach the Downies' house would be along the old railway cutting. If he could force a way through the trees and bushes that grew in it he would be under cover until the moment when he climbed over the garden fence. The question was how to get into the cutting. Almost immediately he saw that he must do it through the tunnel. If he could enter the tunnel at the river end, and if he could make a hole in the second barrier like the hole in the first – a second doorway to the priest's hole – then he could go right through. And the cutting was the last place they would expect him to be, because they wouldn't see how he could have got there.

He had already stopped walking and now he turned round. It was a pity he had been found by the man, otherwise he could have gone back over the railway lines and along the edge of the river. He had to get to the bridge where the woman fed the cats, and he could think of no way except by road. Although he wasn't much good at maps he could see in his mind the road he was on and the road he wanted to be on, making two halves of a V. The bottom of the V was the crossroads by GORDON DOWNIE OK, the point of maximum danger; across the top of the V ran the Ladyhill road, and that was the way he would have to go.

Eleven

It was fortunate that he had his torch with him; he had never taken it out of the zip pocket of his anorak after exploring with Thomas. What he didn't have was any money. He checked very carefully, hoping he might find enough for a packet of crisps, but there was nothing but fluff and anonymous crumbs. He wondered if Mrs Downie would keep his meal for him, or whether she would be too cross when he eventually turned up to let him eat it. He supposed Gordon would have told some story that exonerated him from blame for Philip's absence. 'He went off. He said he didn't want to spend the day with us. He said he'd rather take care of himself until his parents come back.' 'But what will he eat?' 'Oh, I don't know. Buy himself some fish and chips, I expect.'

It was misery to pass a fish and chip place on the Ladyhill road. He could avert his eyes from sweetshop windows, but he couldn't do anything about his nose. He wondered what it was like to die of starvation. 'We're afraid he might be – well, we were by the canal and we heard this splash, and when we looked round he'd gone. We poked about a bit but we couldn't feel anything. I expect he got trapped in the weed.'

Surely he had been walking along the Ladyhill road far too long. The top of the V couldn't be as wide as this; he must have missed his turning. He passed a doctor's surgery, similar to others he had seen in Glasgow: it had the front of an ordinary shop, only the big glass windows had been painted dark green, and instead of a proprietor's name up above there were bold letters spelling SURGERY. Suppose he fainted on the doorstep? 'Nothing wrong with this boy except starvation. Nurse, fetch him a good square meal.'

There was his road at last, and it was downhill all the way to the river bridge. He could actually see the bridge from here, though much of the intervening road was hidden. As he looked he saw two small figures on bicycles ride across it. Although they were too distant for recognition they made him feel uneasy. He walked a little way down the road and then, on an impulse, stepped inside the entrance of a tall stone tenement. It was dark in there and silent; maybe this one was due for demolition and was already empty.

Presently he heard creaking pedals and people breathing hard.

'Are we going along the Ladyhill road?' gasped the voice of Malcolm.

'Yes, we'd better,' said the voice of Robert.

Somewhere above Philip a door slammed, and feet began crashing down the steps. He peered out; Robert and Malcolm had gone by. He began to run down the hill. The Ladyhill road had at least been straight, but this was like the other half of the V, all twists and turns. Each time he rounded a corner he was afraid of what he might see. At last it was the bridge, and as he put one leg over the parapet he heard bicycle bells. He dropped faster than he had intended and dragged himself painfully on to the ledge under the arch.

They paused for a moment on the bridge.

'Not a sign,' said Robert heavily.

'I expect he's miles away by now.' Malcolm sounded the more bad-tempered of the two.

'On we go,' said Robert.

Philip waited a few moments to be sure they were really gone. Then he emerged and started along the river bank, picking his way through the rough grass with more speed than care and not stopping until he was under the canal bridge. Here he paused to wonder whether there was anyone above him keeping watch from the parapet. Picking up a stone he went to the end of the ledge, and keeping just under cover hurled it downstream. It made a big splash. He listened, straining his ears above the sound of water; hearing no alerted cries he risked coming out into the open. He covered the short distance to the mouth of the tunnel very fast, and the darkness received him without mishap.

First he sat down and leaned against the tunnel wall to get his breath back. He became aware of aches and bruises that he had not noticed before. It was an effort to get up and go along to the priest's hole.

The two tea-chests were just as he and Thomas had left them, closing the hole in the first barrier. After he had moved them he saw that there were another pair similarly positioned in the second barrier. These were much harder to shift. He had no hand to hold the torch, and when he laid it on the floor it was almost useless. Eventually he thought of gripping it in his mouth; and pulling his anorak sleeves over his hands to protect them from splinters and jagged edges, he finally managed to get the upper tea-chest moving. It came out with a screech that set his teeth on edge. The lower one still felt firmly wedged, so he left it where it was. He could clamber through the hole he had made.

It occurred to him as he was doing so that there might be a third barrier, or perhaps a succession of them, enclosing a whole row of cells. He flashed the torch ahead of him in a panic, but saw nothing. It turned out to be a straight walk to the end of the tunnel, and soon he was able to put his torch away.

He had never tried to get along the bottom of the cutting before. It wasn't easy. As well as long grass there were thorny bushes, and tough young saplings with branches like whips. Still, the cover was pretty good. And he was nearly home. He thought of the Downies' house as home; perhaps because it was Home with a capital h in the grim game he was playing with the gang. One thing he was certain of – once he got there nothing should drag him out until his parents arrived. He would be ill (he was ill; well, wounded) he would have a violent pain in his stomach, anything – on second thoughts he would eat his lunch first, *then* get the violent pain in his stomach. However cross Mrs Downie was she would surely not throw him out? He pictured the gang howling like wolves in the close, hammering on the door and calling for his blood. He wondered if he was growing slightly delirious.

Only one hazard remained, and that was the road bridge by GORDON DOWNIE OK. Once he had got through that he would be alongside the gardens of the Hilton Avenue flats. As he drew near it he moved more cautiously.

Then, through a screen of leaves, he saw. James and Neil were on the bridge.

'. . . waste of Saturday,' said James.

'If I could just get hold of him – ' said Neil.

They were facing in his general direction, but they weren't looking down. As soon as he had recovered from the shock he began to withdraw. Perhaps rage and disappointment made him careless; at any rate he hadn't gone far when he heard a shout.

'There's someone in the cutting!'

'Hey, Gordon! He's here!'

He ran then, blundering through the obstacles and on into the tunnel, where the darkness soon slowed him to a walk. He didn't use his torch. So long as they weren't sure he was in here he still had a chance. He moved steadily, holding his hands out before him. It seemed an age before he touched the barrier. Groping, he found the hole he had left and somehow floundered through.

He could hear shouts, but he couldn't tell whether they were in the tunnel yet. He flashed his torch for a moment to show him where the tea-chest was, and picked it up. Of course it wouldn't go back into the hole. One part of his brain listened in a surprised way to his dry breathless sobbing as he struggled and struggled. Then he remembered Thomas's trick and turned the tea-chest end on. A narrow gap was left at the top, which meant he heard the gang clearly when they came along the tunnel.

'Philip! Are you there?'

'Come on out!'

'We're going to get you anyway, so you might as well come!' That was Neil.

'Mind what you're doing with those matches,' said Gordon. 'You nearly set light to me then.'

'I keep thinking he'll jump out at us.' Alastair sounded nervous.

'How long *is* this tunnel anyway?'

'Hey, I think I can see – '

'What?' shouted several voices. 'Oh, now the match has gone out!'

'You're supposed to be keeping those matches going,' said Gordon sharply.

'It's not my fault. You blew it out, all shouting like that.'

'Well, get another lit!'

'I'm trying, can't you hear? Malcolm, *what* did you see?'

'Only the end – the place where it's blocked.'

'There!' The match was alight.

'Yes, he's right. This it is.'

'And Philip's not there.'

'I never thought he'd have come in here,' said Robert. 'He knew there was no way through.'

'Where is he, then? Nobody saw him come out of the cutting.'

'He must have been too quick for us.'

'Let's go and have another look in that old mill. He's obviously been there quite often; you could see, quite a path's been worn round that fence-post.'

The voices faded as they withdrew.

After a while Philip dared to switch on his torch. At least he was still free to choose between light and darkness. Larger decisions felt quite beyond him. He sat on a tea-chest from the second barrier until it occurred to him that while they were down by the river they might search the other end of the tunnel. He sprang up immediately and filled the doorway, so that he was shut into the priest's hole on both sides. Then he felt safe.

Twelve

At five o'clock that afternoon Thomas Fearn rang the bell of Philip's flat. Nobody came to the door.

'Not back yet,' said Thomas to himself. 'Oh well. I'll see him on Monday.'

He started home, but before he had gone twenty yards he paused, stood for a moment, and turned round. Moving slowly, he passed Philip's close and entered the one next to it. He paused again; then he knocked firmly on the Downies' front door.

Mrs Downie opened it. She recognized him as one of Gordon's class, though she didn't know his name.

'Is – er – Philip here?' he asked.

'He's away along the canal with Gordon and the rest,' she replied readily. 'I've scarcely seen them all day. If you meet him I wish you'd remind him his parents are due back any time now.'

'Yes. All right,' said Thomas.

When he returned to the street he was walking more slowly than ever. He went in the direction of the canal.

Philip didn't know how long he had been in the priest's hole. His torch battery had given out soon after the gang searched the other end of the tunnel, and his watch hadn't got luminous hands. He thought it might be evening, but he had no way of telling. He didn't dare go out and see. Gordon might have left people on guard in the tunnel – he kept thinking he heard stealthy sounds beyond the barriers – and it would be impossible to move the tea-chests silently.

He wasn't so hungry any more. He was thirsty instead. His last drink had been from the stream in the morning, and even that had been interrupted. He kept thinking about the stream. It was so near the river end of the tunnel. He played with the idea of making a quick dash out to it, but all the while he knew he never would. The priest's hole enclosed him like a shell; it was horrible to him, but it was the place where he had to be. He could no more leave it than an astronaut could leave his rocket in the depths of space. Did rockets stink inside? No, astronauts had special arrangements.

It had not been nearly so bad when he'd had light. He had known the difference then between real sounds and those he imagined. Apart from the searches of the gang there *were* real sounds down here; water dripped, the barriers occasionally creaked. But the little shuffles, the half-caught footstep, the crack that could have been someone's knee . . . ? ALL RIGHT, he shouted inside his head, I'M HERE. COME AND GET ME!

Nobody came. Sometimes he was afraid nobody ever would.

'Hey! Look who's coming! Well well well!'

'Thomas Fearn!'

'Is that all,' said Gordon.

Thomas approached warily, hands in pockets, and met the gang by the swinging tree.

'What are you doing so far from home?' asked Neil with one of his sweetest smiles.

'Looking for Philip.'

'Are you?' Gordon was suddenly alert. 'Where were you thinking of looking?'

'Oh – ' Thomas shrugged. 'Anywhere.'

'Hey, I bet he knows where he is!'

'Let's go with him!'

'That's not a bad idea,' said Gordon.

'What is this?' Thomas looked warier than ever. 'Your mother said he was with you.'

'Was,' said Robert.

'This morning,' said James.

'We've spent the whole day – ' began Neil.

'Shut up,' said Gordon, and to Thomas: 'You said you were coming to look for him?'

'Well, it seems it won't be any good.'

'But you must have had some idea where you'd look?'

'Your mother said – '

'He knows something!' exclaimed James. 'You can tell!'

'Do you?' said Gordon.

Thomas met his eyes. 'That's my business,' he said.

'Now wait a minute,' said Gordon roughly.

'Throw him in the canal!' said Neil, and some of the gang moved forward as though to act on this suggestion at once.

'Stop that! Let him go,' said Gordon. 'One in today is enough.'

'If that's what you did with Philip I'm not surprised he's run away.'

'Listen, clever, it was Philip who did it to Neil!'

'Not on purpose though,' said Gordon. 'He couldn't have planned anything like that.'

'I'm not so sure,' said Neil. 'And I don't see why we shouldn't – ' He looked from Thomas to the canal.

'No,' said Gordon.

'Oh, I don't suppose he knows anything we don't anyway,'

said James. 'He probably thinks that mill is a great big secret.'

Thomas's face flickered.

'Would you have looked there?' asked Gordon directly.

'I might have done.'

'Well, you can save yourself the trouble.'

Thomas said: 'What makes you think he's anywhere round here?'

'We've seen him.'

'We've chased him,' said James. 'Three times.'

Gordon sighed. 'He may have no guts, but he's great at vanishing.'

'Would you have walked across the lock gates?' asked Thomas abruptly.

'Would I – ? Closed lock gates, do you mean?'

'Yes.'

'Well, I never have,' said Gordon cautiously.

'Philip did.'

'*Philip* did? What for?'

'To reach the ladder, so he could get his sister's bear out of the lock.'

'Oh.' Gordon's face showed grudging belief. 'That wasn't bad.'

'Huh.' Neil remained sceptical. 'I suppose you'll say next he's been scampering over lock gates all day, and that's why we've not been able to catch him.'

'I will say if it was me you were after I'd try my hardest to see you didn't catch me,' said Thomas.

'Yes, you might try,' said James scornfully. 'The thing about Philip is, he manages it.'

'Then why don't you give up?'

'Because I can't go home without him!' shouted Gordon. 'It was bad enough trying to explain why he wasn't there for lunch. If his parents come back and he's still not around, my Dad'll skin me!'

'None of us'll look very good when they find he's been gone all day,' said Robert soberly.

'Humph,' said Thomas.

'Oh, *you* needn't worry. You can go home whenever you like,' said Neil. 'And if I were you I'd make it now. Don't push your luck.'

Thomas, on the point of going, looked at Gordon and spoke exclusively to him. 'Will you walk along with me a bit?'

'Oh my,' simpered Neil; but Gordon flicked a savage glance at him and he subsided.

As soon as they were out of earshot of the rest of the gang Gordon said: 'You've got some idea where he is, haven't you.'

'Sort of.'

'You know another place besides the mill?'

'Listen,' said Thomas, 'if you all go away I'll see if I can find him. I'm not saying any more.'

'The others'll not agree to that.'

'You'll have to make them. I'm not bringing him out to be torn to pieces.'

'We don't intend tearing him to pieces, for goodness' sake! If you like I'll make them all promise not to touch him.'

'All right,' said Thomas, 'but I'm still not going to do anything with the whole pack of you on my heels.'

'Oh look here!' said Gordon. 'We've been searching for him all day; you don't really expect us simply to clear off when you say so? How do we know you won't help him to get right away?'

'He won't be wanting to get right away. His parents are due back; he'll want to get home.'

They had nearly reached the road.

'I thought you wanted to get him home,' said Thomas.

'Look,' said Gordon in harassed tones, 'even if I believe you the rest of them won't. I can't make them do just anything, you know.'

'Well, it's up to you – all of you.'

There was a pause. Then Gordon said quickly: 'How about this? I'll come with you myself – but I'll see that none of the rest do.'

'How can you be sure of them if you're not there?'

'I can leave it to Robert.'

After another pause Thomas said: 'All right.'

'They can wait at the end of the towpath here. Will that do?'

'That would be fine,' said Thomas, a little awkward in the face of Gordon's co-operation.

They went back to the others and Gordon explained the arrangement to them. He had been right about what they would or wouldn't accept; their few objections were answered as soon as made by the fact that he would be with Thomas.

'It's our last hope,' said Gordon. 'And we've got to hurry. His parents are probably there by now.'

'We're in trouble anyway,' muttered Neil, 'now that Thomas Fearn knows.'

'No, we're not,' said Gordon. 'He doesn't clipe just for the sake of it.'

'And I don't know all that much,' said Thomas privately, as he and Gordon set off in one direction while Robert herded the rest of the gang in the other. 'How did Neil get into the canal? Was it Philip's fault or not?'

Gordon explained, finishing: 'It was obvious he had known the rope was going to break, and I think it must have been because he'd tried to cut it down. But I don't think he meant it to break while anyone was on it. He did try to warn us – sort of – only we didn't realise he was serious.'

'Which way did he run?'

'The way we're going now. He must have nipped into the old mill, but we didn't know you could get to it then. We found that out later.'

He recounted the story of Philip's appearances, breaking off to say: 'You're going to the mill, then? I hope you do know somewhere else besides that to look?'

'Yes,' said Thomas.

'It was clever of you two, finding a place like this,' said Gordon as they passed the mill.

'Philip found it.'

'He is quite good at some things,' admitted Gordon.

'Yes.'

When they reached the mouth of the tunnel Thomas went inside, and turned to see why Gordon wasn't following.

'We looked in there,' said Gordon flatly.

'There's a place . . .' said Thomas. 'It's hidden. Philip called it a priest's hole.'

Gordon's face lifted, became interested and practical. 'We need matches, then. Have you got any?'

Thomas shook his head. 'I think we can manage if we go slowly and give our eyes a chance. The light does just about reach that far.'

As they moved into the dimness Gordon asked: 'Did Philip find this too?'

'Him and me.'

'Do you come here much?'

'Och no. It's not that sort of place.'

'Would he be able to hear us coming?'

'I don't know. Maybe we should shout – tell him it's all right.'

'Go on then.'

'Why don't you?'

'It's you he'd rather hear.'

'He'll think I've given him away. Here we are now,' said Thomas with relief.

'But we searched right up to this block – both sides.'

'There are two. These tea-chests move.'

'Where? Where do you mean? I can't see a thing.' Gordon's voice was sharp with uneasiness.

'I can do it by feel.'

As the top one came out Gordon said, 'Philip! Are you there? . . . He can't be. It's too quiet.'

'Perhaps he's fainted,' said Thomas stolidly, pulling at the lower tea-chest.

'I hope you don't expect me to go in there and feel arou – a-a-ah!' Gordon's voice gave way to a startled yell, as a bundle of blackness came hurtling at him through the hole Thomas had made. 'Get off me, get off!'

'It's only Philip – Philip, it's all right, it's just me and Gordon, we're not after you!' said Thomas.

Philip, who had not known how to interpret real noises after so many imaginary ones, began to hear properly again. His fierceness went. He stumbled, and Thomas held him up.

Gordon shook himself. 'Let's get back to the light,' he said in a subdued voice.

Philip's mouth was too dry for talking. He reeled between the two of them as they walked, propped first by one and then by the other. When they reached the entrance the late afternoon sunshine was so bright that he stopped and screwed up his eyes.

'You can sit down for a bit,' suggested Thomas.

'Drink,' croaked Philip in reply, and slithered off towards the stream.

The water made him feel quite different. He sat on a damp stone and said: 'I couldn't see my watch. I thought it would be night.'

'I don't know why you call it a priest's hole,' said Gordon. 'Rat's hole would be a better name. You came out like a cornered rat all right.' His smile at Philip had more friendship and less teasing than usual.

'How long were you in there?' said Thomas.

'I don't know – since I was chased along the cutting.'

'But that's hours!' said Gordon. He shook his head. 'I wouldn't stay in there five minutes.'

'I had my torch to begin with.'

'No food, I suppose? Here, have you eaten anything all day?'

'No.'

'Mum had sausages for us – I asked for a picnic; said we didn't want to stop what we were doing – she put them inside rolls. I don't think I finished them.' He felt in his pockets and produced a crumpled paper bag with one inside.

'Cold dog,' said Thomas unexpectedly.

'Where are the others?' asked Philip with his mouth full.

Gordon explained the happenings of the last half hour.

'You were coming to look for me?' Philip's eyes rested on Thomas in some surprise.

'Oh well,' said Thomas awkwardly. 'Yes.'

'He wanted to check that we hadn't torn you to pieces yet,' said Gordon, and Thomas got rather red. 'I suppose that was why you kept on running, because you thought we would?'

'Well, I had bust your rope – and then Neil . . .'

'It was you, then?'

Philip took his turn at explaining while they left the stream and walked on to the mill.

'I'm afraid we know about this,' said Gordon. 'You'll have to write on the door.'

'Once I nearly did.'

'Let's do it now. I've got a bit of chalk.' Gordon felt in his pockets and bounded up the steps. He wrote

P. GRAY T. FEARN OK.

'How's that?'

'Thanks,' said Philip. Thomas was trying not to look pleased.

'I shan't tell anyone about the priest's hole,' said Gordon. 'It's a secret worth keeping.'

They remembered that they were supposed to be hurrying, and increased their pace for a while.

As they passed the swinging tree Philip said: 'I'm sorry about the rope.'

'Oh, we can easily put up another. You'll be quite handy for it if you buy Donna Carnforth's house.'

Philip was bewildered.

'Six Rowan Drive is the house you're going to look at tomorrow, isn't it? Well, it's Donna's house.' (She was a girl in their class.) 'They're moving to Dundee in the holidays. Come and look.'

Philip followed him to the top of the bank. There was the stretch of grass where the little girls had once played, and in the distance he could see the backs of a row of houses.

'Is that Rowan Drive? I thought it was further away.'

'No, that's it. Donna's is one of the middle ones.'

Philip thought about moving. Getting used to a new house was easy; it was learning new surroundings that took the time. This place was a comfortable fit by now. If they moved to Rowan Drive he wouldn't need to feel skinned.

'You see?' said Gordon. 'You'll be able to try the rope any time you want. You might quite enjoy it by yourself.'